FROM THIS DAY FORWARD

ALSO BY WENDY HALLER

*Kiss You Love, Goodbye:
A Poetic Journey Through Life*

Maggie Malone and Her Imagination

Maggie Malone: "I Can Do It All by Myself"

Bad Dreams, Bad Dreams, Go Away

The Flannigan Girls

FROM THIS DAY FORWARD

WENDY HALLER

From This Day Forward
Copyright © 2025 Wendy Haller

Produced and printed by Stillwater River Publications. All rights reserved. Written and produced in the United States of America. This book may not be reproduced or sold in any form without the expressed, written permission of the author and publisher.

Visit our website at
www.StillwaterPress.com
for more information.

First Stillwater River Publications Edition.

ISBN: 978-1-965733-55-4

Library of Congress Control Number: 2025906019

1 2 3 4 5 6 7 8 9 10
Written by Wendy Haller.
Cover photograph by Ivan / Adobe Stock.
Cover & interior design by Matthew St. Jean.
Published by Stillwater River Publications,
West Warwick, RI, USA.

Publisher's Cataloging-in-Publication
(Provided by Cassidy Cataloguing Services, Inc.)

Identifiers: LCCN: 2025906019 | ISBN: 9781965733554
Names: Haller, Wendy, author.
Title: From this day forward / Wendy Haller.
Subjects: LCSH: Newlyweds—Fiction. | Married people—Fiction. | Accidents—Fiction. | Brain—Wounds and injuries—Fiction. | Love—Fiction. | Resilience (Personality trait)—Fiction. | LCGFT: Romance fiction. | BISAC: FICTION / Romance / Contemporary.
Classification: LCC: PS3608.A548299 F76 2025 |
DDC: 813/.6--dc23

The views and opinions expressed in this book are solely those of the author and do not necessarily reflect the views and opinions of the publisher.

This book is dedicated to my husband, Mike.

"You can't go back and change the beginning, but you can start where you are and change the ending."

—C.S. Lewis

CHAPTER ONE

Jay

Jay Ellis, a local police officer, loved the first day of a new school year. He enjoyed driving through town, seeing the kids standing at the bus stop in their new clothes and backpacks, and the smiles on their faces as they excitedly reunited with friends, they hadn't seen all summer. With the bluebird sky and bright sunlight shining down, there was a vibrant buzz in the air. It reminded him of the deep pride he took in his job, knowing he played a role in supporting and connecting the community, and how being part of something bigger than himself gave his work meaning. Being a police officer was more than just a job for Jay—it was who he was at his core, shaping both his identity and his purpose in life.

He started that day exactly how he loved to begin every day—with a trail run through the back woods behind his house, accompanied by his dog, Jake, and his wife, Emmaline. A quick shower, breakfast, and then off to work with a travel mug of coffee in hand. When he arrived at the police station, he greeted his fellow officers with handshakes, waves, or pats on the back. After a quick change and roll call, he was off in his patrol car to protect and serve another day.

It was still early in the morning; the high school students were already at school while the middle schoolers were waiting at the bus stops. Some looked like they had crawled out of bed with their baggy shorts, loose T-shirts, and long hair sticking out from under baseball caps like bird wings. While others, mostly the girls he saw, were all dressed up in ripped jeans, cropped tops, and with every hair perfectly in place.

Jay smiled to himself, thinking back to his younger days. Adulting was hard, but he preferred it over those awkward teenage years. As he drove up and down the neighborhood streets, he waved and beeped his horn to the kids when he came upon a bus stop, even if they didn't wave back.

He reached his right hand over to his cup holder to grab his drink. He almost forgot about the new four-way stop sign they put up at the crossroads of River Road and Grove Street. Replacing his hand back on the steering wheel, he came to a stop. He was the only one at the four-way intersection except for a car coming up on his left. He knew he had the right of way, so he proceeded forward. Jay turned to look at the blue sedan coming toward him. It did not seem to be slowing down. His eyes bore into the driver. Young, female, blond hair, her eyes staring down at the phone in her right hand. The car was going way too fast. Jay stared at her. He laid the palm of his hand on the horn. He heard himself mutter the word stop, as if she could somehow hear him. Suddenly, the girl's head snapped up from her phone and her eyes locked with Jays. The smile on her face faded, replaced by shock and horror, as the front of her Toyota slammed into the back driver's side door of the police car. The impact of both cars caused a horrible metal on metal sound piercing Jay's ears. He felt his car start to spin.

Jay's head hit the driver's side window then bounced off,

before flinging back and hitting the headrest. His body lurched forward, and his left knee jammed into the dashboard. He let out a loud yelp before his forehead hit the steering wheel with a loud thump, and he blacked out.

Sirens? Do I hear sirens? They are so loud. Voices. Who's talking? He heard his name, or maybe he was imagining it. He was trying to blink his eyes open, but the darkness was intense, his head was incredibly heavy. Yes, it was his name and a banging sound. *Please, stop banging.*

"Jay, Jay," he heard a voice and the pulling sound of the door handle, the car door opening. "Jay don't move. There's an ambulance on the way." *Am I trying to move?* He didn't feel his body moving, but his head—maybe just his head. It felt like it was swaying, side to side, not in a physical sense, but like an unsettling motion inside his skull, rocking him back and forth.

"Wha...what happened?" he said, trying to sit himself back. He felt a hand holding him in place.

"Don't move. The EMTs are almost here."

The voice is familiar. Who is that? Jay slowly blinked his eyes open. *Speedometer, gas gauge, police car, driving, girl, texting, crash.*

"Is she okay?" his voice echoed in his head. "The girl. The girl from the other car. Is she okay?" Jay tried to lift his head again, but it felt too heavy. He turned to the left and placed his cheek on the steering wheel and let the dark envelop him. The voice next to him drifted off with the sounds of sirens in the distance.

CHAPTER TWO

Emmaline

Emmaline was running late for work again. At twenty-six, she thought she'd have figured out how to avoid it by now, but somehow, she was always five minutes behind, no matter where she was headed. Despite her best efforts, something always got in her way when she was rushing to leave the house on time. After turning off the lights, she raced through the cozy log cabin toward the front door. She grabbed her oversized leather bag off the back of the couch and began shuffling through it looking for her car keys. "Dammit," she cursed at herself. Her anxiety level increased as she shook the bag listening for the sound of her keys jangling.

The cell phone in her back pocket began to ring. "Am I ever going to get out of this damn house?" she asked herself in frustration. She debated letting it go to voicemail but decided to check the caller ID first. As she pulled her phone out of her pocket she looked down at the screen. She smiled to herself when she saw the number; it was the police station. She clicked the green answer button. "What did you forget?" she asked with a smile on her face.

"Em, it's Lieutenant Bonetti." Her heart caught in her throat, and her hands began to shake. As the wife of a police officer, there was always a hidden fear of the dreaded phone call or officers knocking at the front door.

"Oh my God, what happened? Is he okay? What's going on? What's happened?" Words tumbled out of her mouth. She placed a hand on her stomach as worry began churning, making her queasy.

"Yes, he's okay, Em. He was in a car accident. He's still at the scene. EMT's are with him. He's banged up, but he says he's fine. He is refusing to go to the hospital. I'm calling to let you know in case you want to go get him or I can have someone drive him home. He's at the intersection of River and Grove." Emmaline heard his tone soften as he talked to her. She recognized the switch from professional to personal. Hearing the lieutenant's voice soften helped calm down the butterflies in her stomach a little bit.

"No need. I'm on my way." Emmaline could still hear the lieutenant talking as she hung up the phone and grabbed the keys she saw out of the corner of her eye. They were sitting on the table behind the couch, exactly where she had put them the night before. Jake, their black labrador, stared up at her from the floor as if to ask what happened. She stared at the dog for a second, "I'll be back soon, boy. Don't worry. Dad's okay," she said it to comfort herself more than the dog. She raced out of the house, almost forgetting to close the door, and ran down the front steps over to her Jeep.

Emmaline drove through the small-town streets of New Hartford, Connecticut on her way to Farmington. The scenery outside her window was a blur as she cursed at every red light she hit on the drive. She was normally a patient person in traffic, but not today. It was thirty minutes to Jay but it felt like it was taking her hours to get him. She pressed the phone icon displayed on her dashboard, then she pressed the name Josie, her best friend, and coworker. She listened to the phone ring as she got caught in another red light. "Dammit." Josie's voicemail picked up and her message played. After the beep, Emmaline spoke loudly and quickly into the air of the car. "Josie, it's Em. Jay was in a car accident at work. I'm heading to pick him up, because of course he's refusing to go to the hospital. I won't make it into work today. Can you let everyone know? I'll call you when I have more information. Love ya, bye."

Emmaline pressed the end button on the display with a trembling finger, her hand unsteady as it hovered over the screen.. She took a deep breath and refocused her gaze as she finally approached the accident scene. There were two ambulances, three police cars, and a blue sedan. The side of one of the police cars was smashed in, while the front driver's side of the sedan looked like it had hit a brick wall. Emmaline's heart went out to whoever was driving the other car. She parked her Jeep on the side of the road. As she turned off the car and opened the driver's side door, her body flung back into the seat. "God dammit." She was in such a hurry to get to Jay she forgot to unbuckle her seat belt. She pushed the button on the seatbelt to release the strap.

Her heart was pounding in her chest as she ran by shattered glass and broken pieces of a headlight on the ground. She raced over to the two ambulances. One had the back doors closed; the other was open. Jay was sitting on the tailgate of the second one with an ice pack on his head and a brace on his right knee.

Jay looked up at her as she approached him. "Hey babe, I'm okay." Em quickly moved toward him trying to swallow the tears creeping up. She threw her arms around him. "Hey," he said smoothing the back of her hair. "Really, I'm okay. An egg on my head from where I hit the steering wheel. Nothing a few Advil won't cure." Emmaline pulled out of his arms to take a glimpse at the bump on his head. She grimaced at the size of it. She moved his head side-to-side and looked over the rest of him. She glanced down at his knee and the brace. "Scottie said I probably sprained it. Nothing to worry about."

"We would like to take him to the hospital to be checked out to make sure there are no other injuries and to get an X-ray of his knee." Emmaline noticed a familiar face inside the ambulance. It was Scottie Perino, Jay's best friend since middle school, who was also an EMT. He tilted his head to the side and glanced down at Jay. It was his nonverbal way of saying to her that maybe she could convince Jay to go to the hospital.

"Babe, you should go. Even if it's to have this bump checked out by a doctor or get a quick scan of your knee." She gently touched the hand holding the icepack to his forehead.

"Really, you guys, don't worry. I'm fine. I may need ibuprofen and more ice later. I'll be good to go in a few hours." Emmaline and Scott knew it was no use trying to convince Jay, especially since the department's policy didn't require him to seek medical attention. He was too stubborn to listen to reason. "How about the girl in the other car? Do we know how she is doing? I asked earlier but couldn't get an answer from anyone." Jay turned his eyes up to Scottie and Emmaline watched him wince at the pain of lifting his head. He tried to stand up to face Scott but wavered a little as he got his balance. Emmaline grabbed his elbow to support him.

"You should go to the hospital," Emmaline said with a look of concern on her face. Jay kept his eyes on Scottie waiting for an answer to his question.

"Um..." Scottie cleared his throat. "It looks like she tried to turn the wheel, but not in time. The front of her car slammed into the side of the cruiser, with the driver's side taking the brunt of the impact. She wasn't wearing her seatbelt. She sustained severe injuries in the crash. I'm sorry, buddy...she didn't make it."

"Oh my god," Emmaline cried out, as Jay sat back down on

the tail of the ambulance. She watched Jay's chin drop down to his chest. She knew this would be incredibly hard for him. The last person he had lost was his father, and though he wore a strong exterior for the world to see, deep down he was a sensitive soul. He kept his emotions tightly guarded, never letting them show.

"I saw her. She was staring at her phone and then looked up at me. Our eyes met right before impact," Jay said with a whisper Emmaline almost didn't hear.

"Those new stops signs at the that four-way intersection should have been a stoplight. It is dangerous here, especially for people who aren't aware the signs are there yet." Scottie's tone was clipped with judgment as he jumped down from the ambulance and sat next to Jay. Emmaline could see Jay was trying to process the information. She placed a hand on his back.

"Thanks, Scottie. I think I'll get him home now," she said helping Jay up.

Scottie stood up from the tailgate and began closing one of the back doors. "I would recommend monitoring him overnight for what is most definitely a concussion. Wake him up every few hours to check on him. If he starts to show any signs of headaches, nausea, dizziness, please make sure to bring him to the ER immediately. I know you know this, but I have to tell you anyway. Call me if you need anything." Emmaline watched Scottie as he closed the ambulance doors and walked around toward the front of the vehicle.

As the doors closed, they could see the other ambulance. Through the back windows the figure of an EMT sat next to a gurney. Although they couldn't see the girl, she knew her lifeless body lay inside covered by a thin sheet. The ambulance slowly began to pull away from the scene. They both stood there in silence staring at the back of the vehicle as it drove away.

"I'm so sorry, babe. Are you okay?" Emmaline looked at Jay with the saddest eyes.

"She was a kid. I can't believe she's gone. I can still see the shock in her eyes right before impact—shock, and fear. Oh my god, Em, her family...her parents." Jay was visibly shaken by the loss of the young life. She wanted to get him home so he could rest. Jay, ever the friendly neighborhood police officer, took the time to thank everyone he passed on their way back to her car, despite how she knew he was feeling internally.

CHAPTER THREE

Jay

It was a whirlwind of a day, and all Jay wanted to do was crawl into bed. His head hurt more than he let on and now his heart hurt from finding out the young girl had died in the crash. His knee was throbbing, and he needed to get it elevated with some ice on it. Emmaline helped him up the stairs and down the hall to their bedroom. They lived in a two-story log cabin he had designed and built himself with the help of his buddies a little over five years ago. It had been his dream to have a stone fireplace and to live in a log cabin in the woods.

The house was on a wooded street set back from the road down a long gravel driveway. The cabin butted up against woods and had running trails right out their back door. When he and Em first started dating, he was so proud to bring her back there and show her the house. They both mostly grew up in single mother households with not much money to their names. Owning his own home was a huge accomplishment for him.

Jay gingerly took off his uniform and climbed into bed in his underwear. He wanted to lie in the dark, in the quiet of his home. Jake jumped up on the bed, curling up next to his feet.

"Is it okay for him to be here with you?" Emmaline asked him.

"Yeah, my boy knows when I need some extra comfort." Jay reached down and scratched behind the dog's ear.

"You rest. I'm going to go downstairs and check-in with work, then I'll call our moms and let them know what happened. I'll be up in a bit to check on you. Are you hungry? Do you want something to eat?"

"No, I'm fine. I think I need to sleep for a bit. I'll be good after a nap." Emmaline bent down and kissed him on the lips. She patted Jake on the head and turned the light off on her way out the door.

CHAPTER FOUR

Emmaline

Emmaline texted their friend group to let them know what happened to Jay and how he was doing. She wished he wasn't so hardheaded and had gone to the hospital to be checked on. It would make her feel better if a doctor had seen him. Jay was stubborn when it came to his own well-being, he took care of everyone else but himself. She monitored his symptoms throughout the night. She prepared another set of ice packs for his knee and his head while she called Jay's mom.

Andrea picked up on the third ring. "Emmaline, sweetheart, so nice of you to call. How are you?" Andrea and her second husband, Steve, had moved to Florida for Steve's job when Jay was a senior in high school. Jay stayed in Connecticut with Scottie and his family to finish high school before heading to the police academy. She and Jay were still close despite the geographic distance between them.

"I'm fine; unfortunately, Jay is not." Em bit her bottom lip when she heard the words coming out of her mouth. Not the best way to deliver the news.

"Oh my god, what happened? Is he alright? Did he get shot?" Andrea's voice was getting louder with each question.

"I'm sorry, Andrea, no he's fine. He was in a car accident while in his patrol car. He sustained an injury to his knee and a pretty large egg on his head."

"Holy Jesus, girl, what are you trying to do to me. In my mind, I had a bag packed, and I was boarding a plane." Emmaline heard a long exhale come from the other end of the line.

"Again, I'm so sorry. He's upstairs sleeping. He has a brace for his knee and ice for the swelling. Scottie and I wanted him to go to the hospital, but he refused."

"Of course, he did. He's as pigheaded as his father was."

"I know. I'm going to monitor him overnight. If I even see the slightest wobble, I'll drag him there myself."

"Good. Seriously though. Is he okay?" Emmaline could hear the concern in her voice. She had lost her first husband after a tragic accident at work and Emmaline could only imagine how scary the thought of losing her son to one would be as well.

"Andrea, he was hit by a teenage girl who was texting and driving without her seatbelt on. She didn't make it." Emmaline's voice was barely a whisper when she said the last few words.

"Oh, my goodness, that poor girl. Her family." Andrea grew quiet. Emmaline knew she was taking the time to absorb what she had heard. She stayed silent to give her the space. "Does Jay know?"

"Yes, he knows. I don't think he's processed it fully yet; he was still in shock and a bit frazzled when I brought him home."

"Oh, my sweet boy. This is going to be tough for him. You know how sensitive he is under that strong exterior he hides behind. Do you think I should come up there?"

"Not yet, let's wait and see. I think I'd like to assess his physical injuries before we address the emotional ones."

"Ever the caretaker, my sweet. He is so lucky to have you.

Okay then, keep me posted and when he feels up to it have him call me."

"I will." They said their goodbyes and as she ended the call Emmaline thought about all Jay and his mom had been through in their lives. Jay was a strong, charismatic man with a lot of charm, but underneath it all was a sensitive little boy who still felt the loss of his father.

CHAPTER FIVE

Jay

In between Emmaline's check-ins, Jay slept restlessly through the night. Images from the morning flashed through his mind when he closed his eyes. The expression on the young girl's face, the sound of metal on metal, the feeling of his head bouncing from window to headrest to steering wheel. He knew he'd suffer the repercussions from the accident more the next day than he was in the moment. He also felt a strong need to learn the girl's name. There was something inside him urging him to reach out to her family. He dreamed he was standing before the girl's parents, desperately trying to speak, to apologize, but no words would come out. Her parents were crying, and he felt the sadness radiating from the figures before him. He tried to reach out to comfort them, but his hand dissolved into the air. Suddenly, he felt his shoulder being softly nudged. "Jay, Jay. I'm sorry to wake you. I wanted to check on you." Emmaline was sitting on the edge of the bed, one hand on his shoulder, the other moving a whisp of his hair away from his forehead. He stared up at her in a daze, the memory of the dream disappearing into the back of his mind. "You've been asleep for three hours. I brought you more Advil. Can you sit up a little to take them?"

Jay rolled over onto his back and tried to sit up straight. The weight of his head was too much for him, as if it were a fifty-pound bowling ball. He needed his hands to support him as he rose to a seated position. Em handed him the capsules and a glass of water. He took one at a time from her and then laid back down and closed his eyes.

Jay barely remembered Emmaline waking him up throughout the night to check on him. Moments from the crash and the girl's face haunted him in his sleep. The next thing he was aware of was the annoying alarm sound coming from his cell phone. *Ugh, okay Jay, you can do this. Time to get up and go to work.* His body was stiff as he slowly sat up in bed. His neck hurt, his head hurt, his back hurt. He thought if he could just get his body moving, he'd be okay. Jay pulled himself out of bed and into their bathroom. *A hot shower is exactly what my body needs.*

Twenty minutes later he hobbled down the stairs and over to the kitchen in their open floor plan living space. "Good morning."

Emmaline was stretching out on the floor getting ready to go for her morning trail run. "What are you doing up and dressed? You should be resting."

"I'm going into work," he said matter-of-factly, grabbing his shoes by the door, and slipping his feet into them.

Emmaline stared at him with her eyes wide open in shock. "Oh no you're not. You were in a car accident yesterday. Work will understand if you take today off to rest and recover. Actually, I bet they expect you to take the day off. You still have a huge bump on your head, and you were moaning a lot in your sleep. What about your knee?"

"I'm good. Really, Em. Maybe a little whiplash, but my head doesn't hurt as bad today. There is also less pain in my knee. I probably don't even need this brace." He was exaggerating the truth. His head did still hurt, the lights in the room weren't helping either. He didn't understand why she had to have so many lights turned on when the cabin got so much natural light in the morning.

Jay poured himself another cup of coffee to go in a travel mug he pulled from the dish drainer. He bent down to give her a kiss goodbye, and the bump on his head began to pound with the motion. She stopped him with one hand. "Promise you'll come home if it's too much." He interlaced his fingers in her open palm then pulled her toward him for a kiss.

"Promise. Love you."

"Love you." He gave her one last kiss before heading out the door.

As Jay walked into the station, all eyes turned toward him. He gave a slight nod, as if to greet his coworkers, before heading into the locker room. Not greeting each person as he walked by was unlike him—this wasn't his usual behavior. He knew people had questions about yesterday, but he didn't want to answer them yet. He was nauseous from not eating breakfast and only having half of his morning coffee on the ride over. He grabbed a granola bar from the stash he had at the top of his locker and took a bite. Chewing slowly, his head pounded more and more with each chew. Maybe Emmaline was right; maybe he should have stayed home today.

"Jay, what are you doing here? You should be home." Jay turned and saw Lieutenant Bonetti standing in the doorway of the locker room. Bonetti was a big, burly Black man whose appearance was intimidating to those who didn't know him. Those who did were well aware he was a big teddy bear with a heart of gold.

"I'm good, sir. A little whiplash is all. Nothing a little Advil won't cure," Jay said, grabbing the rest of his stuff and heading out the locker room for roll call.

Lieutenant Bonetti went through the morning roll call with everyone on duty. When he got to Jay, he normally would do a quick inspection as Jay was always prepared for the day. But Jay noticed he lingered longer on him today. He leaned into Jay and whispered in his ear, "You forgot your ticket book." Jay glanced down and realized he was right. It was not like him to forget anything. "Don't worry about it. Go grab it on the way out. Marco will tell you which cruiser you're assigned to today." Jay followed the other officers out of the room internally chastising himself for being careless.

Jay was on duty until four o'clock. As the day progressed, so did his headache. The sun was especially bright, and his sunglasses were not helping. The nausea had not gone away, even after stopping at the deli and grabbing a sandwich. Luckily, it was a slow day spent mostly doing speed checks on the main road. He only pulled one person over for failing to come to a complete stop at a stop sign and not using a turn signal. When he got back to the station, he was so grateful for the day to be over. He quickly packed up his stuff and slipped out without stopping to chat with anyone.

As he walked to his truck, his cell phone rang. He pulled it out of his front pocket and glanced at the number. "Hey, Pino." Pino was the nickname Scottie had been given when they played baseball together. They had played little league baseball together but on different teams. They grew closer once they graduated from elementary to middle school and began going to the same school and playing on the same team. His senior year of high school his mom married Steve; they relocated to Florida for Steve's job. Jay wanted to stay in Connecticut, so he moved in with Scottie's family to finish out the year. Jay considered him more like a brother than a best friend.

"You were in a car accident yesterday. Why the hell are you going to work today? Also, I got a frantic call from your mom wanting to know if you're okay. You should call her." Jay slept away most of the previous night. He didn't think to call anyone.

"I'm sorry, man. I was so out of it. I don't know why she called you. Em called her last night. How did you know I went to work." *This really is a small town.* Jay unlocked his black Ford pick-up truck and climbed inside. His body felt like he was lifting bricks into the truck.

"She was worried about you. She called me wanting to know more details about your injuries. I found out you went to work when I went to the bakery. Dottie was there dropping off a bread order." Dottie Jacobs was Emmaline's mother. Jay and Emmaline didn't realize the strange connection they had until they had been dating for a while. Dottie Jacobs was a baker and worked for Scottie's family bakery until she retired. She now works for them part-time out of her house filling specialty bread orders. Perino's Bakery was one of the last Italian bakeries in the area. All of those years, Dottie worked for the Perinos and not once had Jay, Scottie, or Emmaline run into each other.

"This town never ceases to amaze me. Em calls my mom, who calls you. You see Dottie, who tells you I went to work because Em probably called her to vent about me going in. I'm okay. A bit of a headache and some whiplash. I'm heading home to pop some more Advil." Jay turned the key in the ignition and waited for his phone to switch into Bluetooth mode before backing out of his spot. The sun was shining through the windshield right into his eyes, forcing him to close his eyes for a moment. He was about to say goodbye and hang up when he heard Scottie say something else. "What was that?"

"I'm sorry about the girl. The one who died in the accident. I can't imagine it was easy for you to hear she didn't make it." Jay went quiet for a moment then mumbled a thanks and hung up. He sat in silence for a beat. He was so preoccupied by his day at work and his horrible headache he forgot about the teenage girl. His heart ached recalling the last moments when their eyes met before the crash. He wanted to find out her name. He needed to find out her name. A thought flashed through his mind. *She died, and I didn't.* A wave of guilt washed over him as he put the truck in reverse.

CHAPTER SIX

Emmaline

Emmaline worked at The Village at River's Edge Nursing Home as an LPN. Eventually, she wanted to study for her state boards to become a registered nurse. In the meantime, she took the job at the nursing home because it was where her Aunt Viv was placed when she could no longer care for herself. Emmaline fell in love with the facility and the staff and knew it was the perfect place for her to start her nursing career. She spent the day planning and managing patient care, taking them out for their morning and afternoon strolls, and serving meals. She loved the routine of it and being able to spend special time with each patient in her care. Although today her mind was distracted. She kept thinking of Jay and wondering how he was doing. He would never admit when he was sick. In the three years they had been together, one of them as a married couple, he had only called out sick one time. He was burning up with a fever, and Emmaline threatened to call his lieutenant and tell him that Jay was contagious and would infect everyone at the station.

"Hello. Hello, Em. I'm your patient. Pay attention to me." Emmaline peered over at her Aunt Viv. Her mother's older sister was a sassy old broad or as her mother called her an SOB which could mean different things on different days. She had no filter when talking, but now with her early onset dementia it had gotten worse. "Stop daydreaming about hitting it in the sack with that hottie hubby of yours and get over here and help me out of this godforsaken nightgown. It's practically three in the afternoon and I'm still in my pajamas."

Em shook her head at her aunt. "Viv, it's eleven in the morning and you already changed yourself. You're wearing your day dress."

Viv glanced down at herself and smiled. "Well, I'll be. Look at how fancy I am so early in the morning. Am I going on a date today? Do you think your handsome hunk of a husband would give this old lady a romp in the hay? I bet I have some moves up my sleeve he's not ever done before."

"All right, enough. Come on, it's game time for you in the rec room. I'll walk you down. And my handsome hunk of a husband does not need any advice in the bedroom from you. He does fine on his own." Emmaline walked beside Aunt Viv, leading her toward the recreational room where she would spend the next couple of hours hooting and hollering as she card-sharked the other residents in multiple games of high-low jack.

After sitting her aunt at her game table, Emmaline walked down the hall to get to her next patient. Her best friend, Josie, came whipping around from behind the nurses' station and grabbed her by both arms. "Oh my god, Em. How is Jay? How are you? Your mom came in this morning to have breakfast with Viv and filled me in a little bit. I can't believe Cecelia died. Her poor family. Is Jay okay?" Josie never talked; she rambled on in long run-on sentences.

"You knew her? The girl?" Emmaline stopped in her tracks and stared over at her friend.

"Sort of. Cecelia Downs was a year older than my brother.

He knew her from school. She was a senior this year. I'm so sorry for you guys, Em. How is Jay doing?" Josie asked while fidgeting with whatever was in the pocket of her scrubs.

"He went to work today," Em said with a bitter tone.

"What?"

"I know. He was in this horrible, tragic accident yesterday. Hit his head on the driver's window, the back of the seat, and the steering wheel. His knee rammed into the dashboard. Scottie told me in a text last night that he even blacked out for a few minutes. But he walked away like it was no big deal and then went to work today. The man is made of steel."

"I wouldn't be too sure. His body may still be in shock. You should keep an eye on him, Em. We've seen enough falls around here to know injuries don't often show up right away." Emmaline knew Josie was right. Her gut instinct was telling her Jay still needed to be monitored despite what he said about how he was doing. "Are you still going to trivia tonight after work?"

"No. I'm going to force Jay to stay home by telling him I'm too tired," Emmaline said. The lunch trays were coming down the hall from the kitchen staff. Emmaline and Josie walked down to meet them to begin the lunch rounds.

Josie grabbed a sheet of paper off the lunch cart and began wheeling hers away. "Good idea. Let him think it's you and not him. See you in a bit."

Em and Josie worked a split shift from eleven in the morning to seven at night. Every Tuesday night after their shift ended, they would meet Jay and their group of friends at Mountain Laurel Brewing for trivia night. The brewery was a special place for her and Jay as it was where they first met and fell in love.

As she walked down the hallway with her lunch trays, she

thought about that first night. She had been sitting at a high-top table with Josie and a few of the other girls from work. They had their heads down, answering the questions the emcee had called out. Emmaline was in charge of writing the answers down because her handwriting was the most legible of everyone in the group. Every time she glanced up from the answer sheet her eyes connected with the guy a few tables down from her group. He had mahogany brown hair, the color of chocolate, deep, beautiful brown eyes, and long eyelashes. Even from where she sat, she could see his eyes as his gaze connected with hers.

During the break between round one and two, Emmaline went up to the bar to get the next round of drinks for her table. She felt his presence before he even spoke. "Your table is very animated. You all seem really confident in yourselves. Some of these questions are pretty tricky." She knew he was talking to her even before she turned around.

"Oh, believe me, we know our stuff." Her heart was racing as she tried to keep her cool. He was even more attractive up close. "How about you guys? I hear more arguing over answers coming from your table. Makes me think we have tonight's game in the bag." She was flirting with him, and she could tell he was enjoying it.

"Really, you think so." He smiled at her and the butterflies in her stomach flapped their wings even harder. "How about we bet on it?"

"A bet. What kind of bet?"

"If my team wins, you have to go on a date with me." He placed his hand on the bar next to her so their pinkies were touching. Heat rose to her cheeks.

"O-kay, and if my team wins?"

"I have to go on a date with you." He laughed at his own joke. He was charming, and he knew it.

"Oh really, I think I'd rather make you work for it. How

about this instead? I'll go on a date with you *when* your team wins. Maybe this week, maybe next...who knows?" She shrugged and turned away from him to walk back to her table.

"Wait...I never got your name. I'm Jay, Jay Ellis."

"Emmaline. Emmaline Jacobs." She walked back to her table a little lighter in her steps, completely forgetting to order the round of drinks she went up to the bar for. Her team won that night and for the next four weeks. It became a running joke on Tuesday nights between the two teams, making the competition and magnetic attraction between Jay and Em even stronger. After five weeks of losing, on that sixth Tuesday, Jay's team finally won. After the emcee announced his team as the winners, Jay slapped his hands on the edge of his table, stood up and yelled across the room. "Emmaline Jacobs, you owe me a date." Both teams burst out laughing. Emmaline walked over to Jay with a pen and wrote her phone number on the palm of his hand. That was over three years ago, and he still gave her those same butterflies with one glance from his velvety eyes.

Emmaline walked through the door around seven thirty. One of her patients had bumped into her when she was carrying their bedpan to the toilet and the pee splashed everywhere. She desperately needed a shower.

"Jay, I'm home," she yelled openly into the house. Jake came running down the stairs to greet her, which told her where Jay was. She dropped her bag on the floor and keys on the sofa table behind the brown, leather couch, and headed up to their room.

Emmaline walked into the room. All the lights were off. She could barely make out the shape of Jay laying in their rustic wooden bed. "Jay," she whispered.

"Hey," he said in a muted voice as his head was facedown under a pillow.

"Tough day?"

"You were right. I shouldn't have gone into work today. I already told Bonetti I'd be taking the rest of the week off. He didn't argue at all."

"What hurts?"

"Everything. My body aches, my knee is throbbing, my head is pounding. I shouldn't have gone in today. It was too much."

"How about we go to the hospital and get you looked at."

"No. I only need a few days of rest."

"Jay, please. I'd feel better if a doctor checked you out. They can do a CT scan on your head and an X-Ray on your knee."

"Em, really, I'll be fine. I overdid it today. I'll be fine after a few days at home."

"Okay, but promise me, if your symptoms get worse you will go to the hospital. No arguments."

"Yes and no arguments." He peered over at her with a side smile, and her heart melted. Even in his injured state, he was irresistible. She nodded.

They stayed there for a few minutes in silence. Emmaline tossed and turned in her mind, debating whether or not she should tell him about Cecelia. "Babe, you know the girl from the accident who passed away?"

"Yeah." Jay's head shot up staring at her.

"I found out her name today. Josie knew who she was."

Jay rolled his body fully over and winced as he sat up in bed. He placed a hand over the bump on his head like he was trying to stop the throbbing.

"Her name is Cecelia Downs. She was a senior at Northwestern Regional High School. Josie's brother went to school with her." Emmaline reached over and held one of his hands in hers as she watched his face.

"Do you know..." She watched him pause to swallow down the tears as they were trying to surface. "Do you know when her services will be?"

"I don't. Maybe it's still too soon, but I will find out. Why?"

"I want to go," he said, his voice a little stronger.

"Are you sure, Jay? That might be a lot for you *and* for her parents."

"Em, you don't understand. I need to go. I was the last person to see her alive. I can't get the expression on her face right before impact out of my head. Every time I close my eyes, she's there. I kept dreaming about her and her family last night. In my dreams, I was trying to reach out to them. To talk to them. But something was always blocking it from happening. I don't know why, but I feel connected to them in some way."

"I understand. Or maybe I don't, but if you feel this strongly about it then I'll get the details for her funeral, and we will go together." She leaned over and kissed him gently on the lips. They were still sitting in the dark with only the glow of the hallway light shining into the room.

CHAPTER SEVEN

Jay

Jay woke up in the most uncomfortable position. At some point in the night, he had made his way downstairs and ended up on the couch. His body was contorted, and half his body faced the back of the couch while the other half faced the front. He looked out the kitchen window and saw the sun peeking up over the trees in the backyard. Three quarters of their property was woods; he loved the privacy and loved how he could hit the trails behind their house for his morning run. It took him a second to adjust to the time of day. He had slept most of the past two days giving his body time to recover. During his waking hours, his mind kept flashing to Cecelia Downs's eyes. It was an image he couldn't shake. He glanced out of the kitchen window. The sun was rising over the peaks of the trees which told him it was early morning.

Jay slowly sat up; his headache had subsided. He was still stiff but felt better than the day before. The accident was on Monday. It was Friday. His head was not throbbing as much and his knee wasn't aching anymore. He decided to go out for a run. As he went to put his feet on the floor, he almost stepped on Jake.

Man's best friend. Jake must have slept next to him all night. "Hey boy." Jay reached down and scratched the black lab behind his ears. Jake wagged his tail, hitting the floor with the slapping sound of his tail. "Let me go change and we'll go out for our run."

Jay made his way up the stairs. He tried to be as quiet as possible so as not to wake Emmaline. She was a light sleeper and woke up easily. Jay told her once it was because she was a natural caretaker and was on the ready if someone needed her, even when she was sleeping. He tiptoed into their room and quietly walked over to his dresser.

"Hey." *Didn't work.* "You're up. How are you feeling?" she said sleepily from her side of the bed.

"Much better. I'm going out for a run with Jake. Be back soon." He took out his running clothes from the bottom drawer.

"Give me a minute. I'll go with you," she said, slowly sitting up in bed and yawning the sleep out of herself with a stretch of her arms.

A few minutes later they were on the floor of their living room stretching out next to each other. Jay felt good. This was his normal. A morning run with Emmaline and Jake. This was exactly what he needed.

After warming up, they headed out the back door and over to the trailhead at the back of their yard.

"Babe, it's been a few days for you so let's start off slow. A brisk walk, slow jog and then we'll see if your body is ready for more, okay?"

Jay smiled over at his wife as they increased the pace of their walk. She was such a mother hen. "Yeah, that's fine." His mind wanted him to take off into a run, but he knew she was right. His body needed the time to adjust after being stagnant for the past three days.

As they increased to a light jog, his body responded to the movement with muscle memory. He was still feeling stiff from the accident. With every step, a sharp, pounding sensation hammered at the front of his forehead and pulsed along his temples. He tried to push through and attempted to keep pace with Emmaline, but the pain in his head made it hard for him to focus on following her stride. She glanced back at him a couple of times. He gave her a half smile. His gait was off. He was struggling to get his legs to land right on the ground. After ten minutes of jogging the pain was too much.

"Em," he said breathlessly. "Em, I need to stop." Emmaline turned her head around as she slowed herself down. A look of concern washed over her face.

"Of course. Are you okay? Does something hurt? Your knee? Your head?"

"All of the above." Jay bent over, placing his hands on his knees as he caught his breath.

"Jay, maybe it's time you go see a doctor."

"No, no. It was too soon. I should have started out with a brisk walk today and built myself up."

"I really think it would be best if we got you checked out. What if there is something more wrong with your knee?" Emmaline had walked over to Jay, rubbing his back with small circles of her hand.

"No," he said slowly standing up. "I'm okay. I tried to do too much too soon."

"Jay, please," she pleaded with him.

He reached over and placed a gentle kiss on her forehead. "Let me give it the weekend. If there's no improvement by Monday, then I'll go."

"Promise."

"Promise." He took her hand in his and they walked back to the house together with Jake by their side.

Over the next few days, Jay noticed himself struggling more and not only with the headaches. On Saturday, he was unloading the dishwasher, pulled out a fork and stared at it. He looked around the room. He was drawing a blank. The light in the room from the windows and the overhead was too bright. He couldn't concentrate. He couldn't remember where the fork went in the kitchen. He stared at the utensil and then around at all the drawers. He oscillated his gaze around the room while mentally reaching into his brain to recall where the utensil went. He had to open and close a few drawers until he found the right one. He then turned off the kitchen light and pulled the window blinds down.

When he woke up on Sunday morning, he walked into the second bedroom thinking it was the bathroom, even though they had a bathroom in the bedroom suite. When he walked down the stairs to get coffee, his depth perception was off, and he slipped down the last three. He grabbed at his knee as he winced in pain. Throughout the weekend, small things kept happening like forgetting where they kept the dog food, slurring his speech or being unable to complete sentences, but he brushed them off. He didn't share any of this with Em because he didn't want her to worry.

A week had gone by since the accident and his headaches had become migraines. Immediately following the accident, he was sleeping all the time and it had changed to him struggling to sleep. Between the pain in his head and the nightmares, he found himself waking up frequently throughout the night. He couldn't escape the image of Cecelia's shocked face as their eyes met just before the crash. Her expression haunted him, knowing those were the last moments of her life.

He woke on Monday morning in a cold sweat from another nightmare and his head was pounding. Since he couldn't go back to sleep and he still wasn't running, he decided to get into work early. It felt so good to put his uniform back on and get back to somewhat of a daily routine. At work, he said hellos quickly to his co-workers and limited the small talk. He still wasn't ready to discuss the accident and, out of respect, his colleagues did not ask. As Jay walked over to the police car he was assigned, his heart began to race. *Am I ready for this?* He opened the door and climbed in behind the wheel. He took a few moments to gather himself before turning on the car.

Jay drove around town cautiously. He took extra time at all stop signs and even stoplights, fully knowing no one would beep at a police car to get it to move.

At one point he pulled an elderly woman over, he walked up to her window as she was rolling it down. "Hi, Officer. Did I do something wrong?" she asked. Jay looked at her and then up and around the top of the car. He realized he couldn't remember why he had pulled her over. The thought was there but by the time he walked from the patrol car to her, he had completely forgotten. The sun's rays hurt his eyes, he had to squint to try and dim its piercing glow which only made the pain in his head worsen. He turned around and saw a stop sign.

"Um...make sure you come to a complete stop at the stop sign and look for other cars before proceeding." He didn't know if that was why he pulled her over.

"Oh, okay, Officer. Thank you," she said as she pressed the automatic button for her window to roll back up. Jay walked back to his vehicle trying to blink the fog away. The sun was shining brightly. His head was hurting again. At the end of his shift, he was happy to be back at the station. He made a few mistakes on his end-of-day report, which Lieutenant Bonetti would email him about the next day. Jay did not make mistakes. He was struggling and he knew it.

As he got into his truck to go home, his phone pinged with a text. He pulled his cell out of his front pocket and glanced down.

Scottie: Checking in to see how you're doing?

Jay: Hanging in there.

Scottie: Think you'll be up for trivia tomorrow night?

Jay: You bet.

From the first night they met, Jay and Emmaline went to trivia every Tuesday night at Mountain Laurel Brewing with their group of friends. They had been going for so long, at this point, the owners and other patrons were like extended family to all of them. Jay turned the key in the ignition and waited for his phone to switch into Bluetooth mode before backing out of his spot.

Scottie: Are you sure you are up for it?

Jay: Yeah, I'm fine.

Scottie: Great, see you then.

CHAPTER EIGHT

Emmaline

Tuesday afternoon, Emmaline and Josie were standing at the nurses' station at work waiting for the lunch trays to come down the hall from the kitchen staff.

"Are you going to trivia tonight?" Josie asked as she fiddled around with her large hoop earrings. They were earrings she had been told multiple times not to wear to work because a patient could easily pull them out. Some of their patients could be a bit touchy-feely, so their boss had asked all the employees not to wear earrings or necklaces, especially around Viv. When she was confused, she could become aggressive if she saw something she wanted.

"I am planning to," Emmaline said. Emmaline and Josie walked down to meet the lunch trays so they could begin their rounds. "I guess unless Jay says otherwise, we'll meet the crew there as usual."

Josie grabbed a sheet of paper off the lunch cart and began wheeling hers away. "Sounds good. See you in a bit." Josie headed down one hallway with her cart, while Emmaline headed in the other direction. Her thoughts went to Jay as she readied the lunches for delivery. She observed some changes in him since the accident. She noticed he was having trouble sleeping now, whereas, last week he was sleeping all of the time. He tossed and turned in bed next to her, while she tried to sleep. When he was sleeping, he was moaning in pain. He was sensitive to lights. He kept complaining to her that the lights were turned up too bright, even though they were not on a dimmer; they couldn't be adjusted, and nothing was different about them. She also saw him struggling to recall words. She knew she would also forget words from time to time, but this was unlike Jay. They had taken a couple of walks together over the weekend and she noticed his gait was off. She wasn't sure if it was because his knee was still bothering him or not. She was worried and she didn't want to press him. She expected him to know his own body. Suddenly her phone pinged in the pocket of her scrubs. She pulled it out and saw her mother-in-law's name on the text.

Andrea: How's my boy doing?

Emmaline: Were you just in my thoughts?

Andrea: Mother's intuition.

Emmaline: I'm worried about him. I don't like the symptoms I'm seeing.

Andrea: Is he still refusing to go to the doctor?

Emmaline: Yup

Andrea: I'll pull the mom card on him.

Emmaline: LOL. Whatever will work. Maybe

I'm too close to him and this profession and I'm seeing more than what's there. It would make me feel better if you reached out to him.

Andrea: Don't worry, sweetheart. A good guilt trip from mom is usually the tipping point.

Emmaline: TY

Andrea sent back a smiling emoji with hearts for eyes. Hopefully, Andrea would be able to talk some sense into him. Even if it's just for a doctor to confirm he needs time to rest and recover, it would bring her comfort to hear it from a professional, rather than watching him struggle the way he was. *Maybe I've been around too many patients with concussions so I'm looking to see the signs in Jay I've seen in others.*

Emmaline decided it was time to get back to work and stop overthinking for now. She put her phone back in her scrubs pocket knowing she would have some angry patients if she didn't get lunch served to them soon.

When Em and Josie got to the bar, she glanced around for Jay, Scottie, and their other friends. She and Jay still played against each other, but now they sat at tables side by side. She found them on the far side of the room. Jay was in the corner. She could see he was shielding his eyes from the florescent light hanging over his table. He could pretend all he wanted, but she could tell his headache was back. She had texted him a few times during the day asking him how he was doing and each time all she got was a one-word response, *okay, fine,* and *good.*

She walked over to where he was and gave him a kiss on the

cheek. When she looked up, Scottie was staring at her. She met his gaze. Scottie shook his head then nodded toward Jay. She knew what he was saying without him having to say it. Jay was not doing well.

"Hey babe, I'm not feeling great tonight. Would it be okay if we skipped trivia? I think I need to go home. Maybe get to bed early." Jay's eyes lifted to meet her gaze, and she could see his relief. She couldn't tell if he knew she was fibbing for his sake, but it didn't matter. He stood right up.

"Of course. Hey Scottie, can you give Josie a ride back to her car." Scottie agreed and she and Jay walked out of the brewery to his truck. He pulled his keys from his right front pocket. She reached over and took them from him. He didn't argue. They could pick her car up in the morning.

As soon as they got home, he walked over to the couch and laid down. "I can't seem to shake these headaches."

Jake was standing at Em's feet wagging his tail excited about his people being home. "Rest now. I'm going to let Jake out and then make something for dinner. Are you hungry for anything in particular?"

"No. I'm not hungry at all. I'm going to shut my eyes for a few minutes." Emmaline watched Jay bury his head into one of the navy blue, corduroy throw pillows on the couch. She went out the back door with Jake and threw his tennis ball for him. When they came back inside the house fifteen minutes later, Jay was fast asleep. He stayed there all night. Em didn't even try to wake him up when she went to bed. Her worry was growing; she knew the signs of a concussion and he was showing too many of them. Regardless of what Jay said, if he wasn't better by morning she was taking him to the hospital.

CHAPTER NINE

Jay

Jay lied to Emmaline the next morning. He told her he was fine as he rushed out the door for work. Josie had texted them and said she could pick up Emmaline and bring her to her car. He didn't want to spend too much time there as her concerned eyes followed him around the house.

As the day progressed, his headache returned in full force. This one worse than the one from the day before. He was sitting in his patrol car at a school zone which was known for having issues with people speeding, especially while school was in session. He loved to sit in his car and watch the oncoming cars speeding until they saw his cruiser and immediately put on the brakes to slow themselves down like he didn't see them. He pulled out his radar gun, lifting it up to the edge of the window, aiming it at the oncoming cars. He was having trouble keeping it steady. When he gripped the gun, it trembled in his shaky hands. He decided to use the edge of the window for stability. Jay was totally out of sorts between the headache and his trembling hands. He was having trouble concentrating from all the stimuli around him.

Suddenly, a crackling came in over the radio. It was a call from dispatch. There was a domestic disturbance he was being told to respond to. Jay put the radar gun down on the passenger seat. He let dispatch know he was on his way and turned on the lights and siren. The sound of the sirens was too much for him. A flash of white beamed behind his eyes, and nausea overtook him, the pounding in his head was so intense. He was going to be sick. Jay flung open the driver's side door and vomited onto the ground. He quickly reached over to turn off the lights and siren. It didn't help. He heaved out the side of the car again. *Something is wrong.* Jay grabbed his radio and told dispatch he couldn't take the call. Dispatch came back with a worried response. He recognized the voice. *Whose was it?* He was too disoriented to respond. His head was spinning. He grabbed his cell phone from the middle console and hit Emmaline's number.

"Hey babe, how's your day going?" she said in her loving voice.

"Em, something's wrong." He told her what happened as he sat with the phone to one ear and his head resting in his other hand. He was sitting in the driver's seat with his legs hanging outside the car. She asked him where he was. He heard himself say the intersection of Red Oak Hill Road and Meadow Road, but his voice sounded like an echo in his head.

He remembered her arriving. He recalled looking up to see another cruiser pull up next to his. Emmaline was talking to two of his colleagues, but he was too disoriented to understand what they were saying. He heard Em say, "Okay, thanks, guys," before she helped him over to her car. He felt the same way during the accident, like someone was taking snapshots with a camera—flashing images in his head.

Em's mom, Dottie, met them in the reception area at UConn Medical Center. Jay was confused when he saw her walk over to them with a man in blue scrubs. "Jay, this is Jim Gottlieb. Dr. Jim. He's an old friend of mine."

"Nice to meet you, Jay." Dr. Gottlieb held his hand out to shake Jay's, and he returned the gesture. He was a bit confused about what was happening. He wanted to sit down and close his eyes. He saw an open seat across the lobby and made his way over, leaving the three of them standing there talking amongst themselves. He heard Dr. Gottlieb say something about a CT scan, not an MRI, because the noise would be too much. Em came over and guided Jay out of the chair and down some hallways with lights so bright he had to cover his eyes. She walked him into an exam area and helped him change out of his clothes into a hospital gown.

Nurses, orderlies, people came in and out of the room as he lay on the gurney with his head burrowed in the blanket and his eyes closed. Someone had thankfully turned the light in the area off. He could hear Emmaline talking on her cell phone. It sounded to him like she was talking to Scottie or maybe his mom. Even though she was talking quietly, in his head it sounded like she was yelling.

"Hi Jay, I'm Tom. I'm going to take you for your CT scan. I put an extra pillow by your side if you want to use it to cover your eyes for the ride down the hallways." Jay heard the brake on the bed unlock and felt himself begin to move. He started to become nauseous again. He grabbed the extra pillow Tom had brought him and covered his face with it.

The next couple of hours were a blur. He was put in a machine, given an IV with medication that helped his migraine, and brought back to the room where Emmaline had been waiting.

"Hey babe, how are you?" She asked as she gently swept her hand across his forehead along his hairline.

"I don't even know. I can't seem to focus. Everything is hazy." As he was trying to turn his head to look at her, Dr. Jim came into the curtained room, holding an iPad.

"Jay, Em," he acknowledged both of them as he glanced up from the screen. "How are you, Jay?"

"I've been better."

"I'm sure." Dr. Jim pulled up a scan on his iPad and turned it around for Jay and Emmaline to see the image. "Jay, Dottie filled me in on your car accident. I want to ask you, have you had concussions in the past?"

"Yes, a few from playing sports in high school. I took a baseball to the temple during practice and was knocked out, that was probably the worst one. Why?"

"Based on the images we took today, the extent to which you hit your head the day of the accident and past trauma, you have sustained a traumatic brain injury. See this area in here." Dr. Jim pointed to a cloudy area on the screen and continued to talk in language Jay didn't quite understand. "Since the accident, have you noticed any changes? Sensitivity to light or sound? Trouble recalling information or confusion?"

"Some." Jay did not elaborate so Emmaline filled in the information for him.

"I've noticed he's more sensitive to light. He's commented a few times about how bright our house is when the lights are turned on. He tried to go out for a run, but it was too much for him. I'm not sure if it was the pounding of his feet on the ground or the movement itself."

"Could be both," Dr. Jim replied.

"So, what does this mean for him? What is the treatment for a traumatic brain injury?" Emmaline reached over to hold Jay's hand. He didn't give it to her, instead he buried it further into the thin sheet covering him. He was too uncomfortable in his body to be touched. She rested her hand on top of the blanket instead, trying not to show how taken aback she was by his withdrawal.

"Well, it's hard to know the full extent of a TBI. The brain takes time to show all of its symptoms, as well as time to recover. We can give you medicine for the headaches to start with. Then I'd like you to schedule an appointment with my office for further testing. I'd really like to do an MRI once your migraine has subsided so we can see the full spectrum of the trauma. Then we can work with our team to create a treatment plan for you." Dr. Jim was directing all this to Jay who was trying to absorb everything the doctor was saying.

"No meds," Jay said emphatically. Dr. Jim peered over the top of his reading glasses sitting on the edge of his nose.

"His father had a problem with addiction," Emmaline explained softly under her breath.

"Well, we can give you something non-addictive. Like a beta blocker to help ease the pain."

"No meds," Jay said firmly.

"O-kay," the doctor sighed, "then let's start with some lifestyle changes and an appointment with my office for some additional testing. We want to monitor your symptoms, see how extensive the injury is, and make a treatment plan for you. You might want to think about taking some time off of work until the migraines subside—"

"Not going to happen," Jay interrupted.

"If you're symptoms increase, you're going to need to Jay. Any signs of a delay in cognition, memory recall, problems with balance, you're not going to be able to continue in your role as a police officer. It's not safe for you or the community." Those words hit Jay like a knife to the heart. He did not respond. Not being able to do his job, like he couldn't that day, was something Jay had never dealt with before. "In the meantime, get plenty of sleep, take daily walks, get fresh air, stretch, avoid caffeine, and over the counter meds for the pain for now. Jay, we have a great team of therapists who can really help you if you let them." Dr. Jim typed a few notes into the iPad, said his goodbyes and excused himself from the room.

Jay hadn't realized Dottie had been standing at the door. She touched the doctor's arm as he walked out as a gesture of thanks and then walked into the room and over to Jay. "Jim is a great guy and a great doctor. He can really help you. I've seen him work miracles with his patients."

Jay looked up at Dottie. "I'll figure it out. I'll be okay. I don't want any prescription pills and I'm not giving up work."

"Babe, we know your aversion for prescription drugs. I know your dad was on really heavy pain meds and became addicted, but that doesn't mean you will be. Beta blockers are non-addictive and can be a tremendous help with headaches and anxiety. Not saying you have to decide now, but please keep it in mind if you think you need it."

"Don't nurse me, Em. I'm fine." His words were sharp, and he could see they visibly stabbed Emmaline as he saw the hurt in her eyes. "Can we go home?" He began to sit up forgetting about the IV in his arm.

"Jay, wait. I'll go get someone." He watched Dottie make eye contact with Em and then leave the room. Emmaline had been holding his bag of clothes. She started to take them out and hand each piece to him. He knew he should apologize to her, but right now he wanted to get dressed and get the hell out of the hospital. He had too many bad memories of the trips he and his mom would take to visit his dad after his work accident and multiple back surgeries.

CHAPTER TEN

Emmaline

Emmaline and Jay barely spoke on the ride home. She could not even imagine what was going through his head. He was always so strong, so together, everyone's go-to person. His heart was as big as his personality. She knew she was going to have to tread lightly with convincing him to take medication if he needed it. As soon as they walked through the front door, he headed upstairs to their bedroom. He didn't even acknowledge Jake. The nurse in her wanted to immediately call and set up the appointment at Dr. Jim's office to get his treatment plan in motion. She had to restrain herself as she could tell he wasn't ready. He needed time to process everything the doctor told him. Instead, she decided to call Lieutenant Bonetti and give him an update on Jay. The lieutenant had left her a message while they were at the hospital checking up on Jay and she figured the least she could do was to return his call.

"Lieutenant Bonetti," he answered on the second ring.

"Hi Lieutenant, it's Emmaline."

"Hey, Em. How's our guy doing?" She could hear him shuffling around some papers through the phone.

"He's stubborn. But we already knew that. The doctor said he sustained a traumatic brain injury. He had already had a few concussions from previous sports injuries, and it seems the injuries he sustained from the accident did more damage. The doctor wants to do an MRI once Jay's migraine subsides. Once they have the results, he will need to meet with a team of therapists to create a treatment plan. It will change and be adjusted as symptoms present themselves. Unfortunately, this is the kind of injury where the symptoms don't appear overnight. He's refusing medication for the pain. I know you are aware of his dad's history with pills. I'm hoping he will come around because he's in a lot of pain right now and Advil is not cutting it."

"Wow, poor guy. What can we do? How can we help support you?" he asked. Em loved the guys on the force. They were family. A brotherhood/sisterhood who showed up for each other. Their job was a risky one and rewarding one on so many levels.

"His doctor recommended he take some time off from work to give himself time to heal. Jay—"

Lieutenant Bonetti cut her off. "That's a good idea. I can reach out to our human resource department to find out what the next steps will be. It happened during work hours so he will still get compensated. We want our guy to get better. Whatever we can do."

Emmaline was struggling to gather her thoughts; she lowered herself onto the couch. "He doesn't want to take time off. He shut the idea down almost as quickly as he did with the suggestion of painkillers. The doctor did tell him if there was any decline in his cognitive abilities he would have to take a leave of absence from work."

"Oh Em. I'm so sorry for you guys. I'm not going to lie. I have noticed some changes in him. Forgetting things, errors in his reports. He's lost his zest, his spirit."

"I know. I see it all too." Emmaline lowered her voice to

almost a whisper. "Can you make me a promise? Will you please let me know if it gets too bad at work? I don't know if going out on medical leave is a decision he will be able to make for himself."

"You bet. We'll look out for him. Please, let us know if there is anything else we can do to help you out."

"Thank you." She ended the call and sat quietly on the couch for a few minutes with her phone in her hand. She'd supported TBI patients at the nursing home, but not anyone as young as Jay. She glanced around the cabin trying to think of what she could do to help him. She felt so useless. Instead of calling, she decided to text Jay's mom to give her an update. She wasn't ready to talk.

Emmaline: We just got home from the hospital.

Andrea: And?

Emmaline: He sustained a traumatic brain injury. Doctor wants to run an MRI when Jay's migraine subsides. They had him on a magnesium IV drip in the hospital, but he refused meds. Advil is not going to be enough.

Andrea: I am so sorry for you both. One incident can change the trajectory of your life. Unfortunately, we both know this all too well. His dad was an amazing father, but after the steel beam fell on his back, he was never the same. I'm sure that has been in the back of Jay's mind even if he hasn't mentioned it.

Emmaline: The only thing that came up during his visit was his dad's addiction to pain meds.

Andrea: It was a really tough time for Jay. His dad was his world and to watch him suffer and then fall into addiction was hard for a young boy. You will figure it out. You will. In the meantime, I'm here for you. I love you both. I'll call and check in on him later. Please remember to take care of yourself too.

Emmaline: I would like to take care of him if he'd let me.

Andrea: I know, sweetheart, he can be bullheaded.

Andrea finished their texting exchange with a heart emoji. Emmaline was a caretaker; it was what she did for a living and who she was as a person. It was breaking her heart that she couldn't care for her own husband. She knew Jay had a long road ahead of him, but she also could tell he had no idea what challenges were coming his way. She had seen it many times with her own patients. Emmaline placed her phone down on the couch and leaned over touching her forehead to Jake's forehead. He had been sitting on the floor next to her leg as if to say, *I'm here for you.* Em began to cry quiet tears into the space between Jake's soft, black ears. Her heart was aching. In that moment, as she held onto their loving companion, weeping, she knew their lives were never going to be the same.

CHAPTER ELEVEN

Jay

Saturday was Cecelia Downs funeral. Being at the wake was something Jay needed to do. He wanted to see her family, spend a moment in the world of her people and mourn with them. He grappled with survivor's guilt, unable to shake the image of her face and the moment of impact that haunted his dreams. Jay walked down the stairs in his police uniform. He felt Emmaline scan his outfit with her eyes. "Babe, I don't know if you should wear your uniform today. I know you usually wear it to funerals as a sign of respect, but it might be too difficult for the family." Jay stared down at his uniform as he descended the last two steps. It hadn't even occurred to him to wear anything else. He turned around and walked back up the stairs. He had so much anxiety about this day since he found out about the funeral arrangements. Jay had been extra quiet since Tuesday night. He was still going to work, dealing with the pain in his head and in his heart. He hadn't talked about everything going on within himself with Em. It wasn't in his nature to share his deepest feelings, having always relied on the professional wall of a police officer, but Emmaline was the one person he felt he could open up to. She had told him over the last couple of weeks how she hoped he did not feel guilty about the accident as it wasn't his fault. He knew she was trying to get him to talk to her, but he wasn't ready. It wasn't only guilt. It was something else, a deep sadness for both Cecelia and him. He couldn't figure out how to process Cecelia Downs death while dealing with the changes affecting him. His brain wasn't working right. He was struggling more each day.

"Better?" he asked as he came down the stairs again, this time in a black suit with a textured, black tie.

He watched Emmaline's eyes drop to the floor. She had never seen him in a suit. She raised her eyes up to meet his; they were filled with so much sadness. "Yes. You look really nice." She walked over to him and wrapped her arms under his, resting her head on his chest in her favorite spot. Emmaline held him in her arms, but her loving hug did nothing to ease his sadness. He only half returned the hug.

"We should go," he said giving her back a gentle pat.

He grabbed the keys to his truck off the key hook by the door. He reached his hand behind him; Em walked up to him and took his hand. Less words today was what he needed.

They arrived at the funeral home ten minutes later. He approached the door apprehensively not knowing what to expect. On the one hand, he prayed they did not have an open casket. He thought it would break him. On the other hand, maybe it would replace the last images of the young girl's face, the one he saw right before the crash. The expression of fear and shock on her face still lingered in his mind whenever he closed his eyes. Emmaline walked ahead of him. It gave him the courage to put one foot in front of the other. An employee of the funeral home held the door open for them. As they walked through the door there was a slideshow of images of the teenager on a screen in front of them and posterboards propped up on easels off to the side. The pictures showed Cecelia from infancy to her teen years. Em weaved her arm through Jay's, and they took a step forward. This is what they needed to do. Keep putting one foot in front of the other.

Emmaline signed the guest book. They got in line to pay their respects. As they moved along in the line, Jay could sense eyes on them from the other mourners. The town was a decent size but not so big to not recognize Jay as the police officer who was in the car accident with Cecelia. Jay's body stiffened. It was an open casket. Jay stared at the soft features of the girl's face, a sense of peace settled over her, so different from the last image of Cecelia he carried in his mind. Her lifeless body encased in the satin of the coffin. He stared at her soft blond hair as it cascaded over her shoulders, the pale skin of her face. A heart shaped necklace around her neck. She looked like the girl from the accident, but also, she didn't. He wished he could see her eyes. His last memory was of her eyes filled with shock and fear. He felt Em grab at his elbow and guide him to the receiving line.

Jay avoided making eye contact with anyone. He followed Emmaline's feet as they moved up in line. Jay's anxiety was making his heart race in his chest. He didn't know if Cecelia's parents wanted him there or if his being there would upset them more. His mind was racing with self-deprecating thoughts. When it was their turn to pay their respects, Cecelia's mom pulled Jay into a hug. Jay's eyes immediately welled with tears. "I'm sorry, I'm so sorry," he said into her shoulder. Mrs. Downs was almost a foot shorter than him, but she held him like a mother comforting a young child. Mr. Downs came to his other side and put an arm around him while hugging his wife. The three of them stood in a circle of grief which no one else in the room would ever be able to understand. Mrs. Downs quietly comforted Jay.

The three pulled away from each other. "A tragic accident. A tragedy we will never get over," Mr. Downs said as he pulled a handkerchief out of his inside suit pocket and wiped his eyes. "Son, we are so sorry for what you are going through. We know this can't be easy for you either." Jay had no words to give in return, he shook the man's hand instead. Jay and Emmaline slowly walked away from them to pay their respects to the other family members. They sat in chairs at the back of the room for about fifteen minutes. It was too much for Jay; he felt like all eyes were on him, the survivor, more than on Cecelia and her family.

He reached over and squeezed Emmaline's hand to cue her he was ready to go. They walked out of the funeral home nodding at others as they walked by. Once inside Jay's truck, Emmaline glanced over at him as he leaned over the steering wheel. He felt Emmaline place a hand on his back. He turned his body toward her and fell into her lap, sobbing uncontrollably. She had never seen him cry before. He felt her fold herself over his body and together they mourned for Cecelia and the life she would never have.

Once home, Jay took Jake into the backyard and disappeared into the woods. He knew Emmaline understood he needed time to himself. He was grateful for her instinct to let him be alone. He needed time to come to terms with all that had happened over the last couple of weeks in his life. He walked through the woods with Jake at the lead. His head was pounding. He was struggling to keep his eyes open due to the throbbing in his head and behind his eyes. He finally sat down and leaned against a tree. Jake came over and sat by his side. Realization hit Jay. There was no way he was going to be the same again.

CHAPTER TWELVE

Emmaline

The next few weeks were difficult for them. Emmaline could see Jay struggling with simple daily activities. She noticed his balance was off when he got dressed and he had to sit on the bed to put his pants on. He battled with his depth perception while walking up and down the stairs. His irritability and frustration were getting worse, and he was snapping at her more. She tried to keep their days as routine as possible. She invited him to do morning stretches with her before her run. He had no interest. She laid out all the pieces to his uniform the night before so he wouldn't forget anything, and he barked at her how he could do it himself. She tried making him tea in the morning and he dumped it out and made himself coffee instead. She asked him if he would take walks with her and Jake after dinner and he turned her down. He would, however, take Jake out back and sit in a chair throwing a tennis ball for him instead.

After dinner one night, she was washing the dishes and staring at Jay through the kitchen window in the back yard. He was standing in one spot in the yard staring off in the distance with a blank expression on his face. Jake would bring him the tennis ball and drop it at Jay's feet. Jay would pick it up and throw it for him, but the joy and laughter was no longer there. The warmth, the love he exuded for those around him was gone. She remembered the first time they hugged. It was at the end of their first date. He had walked her to the door of her childhood home. She felt flutters in her belly like a schoolgirl. She waited for him to kiss her goodnight, but instead he stepped forward and pulled her into his arms. It was a gesture she wasn't expecting. She turned her head to the left as he hugged her, and her head fit perfectly in the space between his shoulder and collarbone. She didn't know why, but tears welled up in her eyes. Then he slowly stepped back, interlaced the fingers of her hands in his, leaned over and gently kissed her. She knew in that moment she had found her place, her home. He was the one she wanted to spend the rest of her life holding hands with. She missed the old Jay. She missed his laugh, his smile, his touch. She knew he was in pain and wouldn't admit to it. He was slipping away, and she felt helpless.

They tried going to trivia night the week after his trip to the hospital. She could see him struggling to answer the questions. Jay was normally a wealth of knowledge when it came to useless facts. He was the strongest member on his team. Every time she glanced over at his table, she could see frustration on his face and concern on Scottie's. She had an idea. Emmaline decided to have their group of friends to the house for game night instead of at the brewery the following week. Maybe less stimuli would be better for Jay. She sent a text out to their group chat inviting everyone over the following week for a potluck dinner and game night. Jay hearted her text which was confirmation to her he liked the idea.

The following Tuesday morning, she got the house ready and prepared a lasagna she could put in the oven after work. She pulled out an assortment of games they had on the top shelf of their coat closet and put them on the coffee table. She noticed Jake had been following her around the house. "Well, boy, let's hope this works. Your daddy could really use some cheering up."

Everyone arrived by seven thirty, eight friends in total, which made for even teams. Platters of food and drinks were spread across the kitchen island and counters. Food and friends, voices in the air. Smiles and laughter, exactly what Emmaline wanted for the night. She caught Jay out of the corner of her eye and saw him laughing while taking a bite of food. She felt hope for the first time in a while. His eyes were lit up with a smile like the old Jay.

After dinner, they started a round of charades. Guys versus girls. Josie was the best at acting out clues as she was very animated in her silent descriptions. Tracy, one of the nurses they worked with, kept talking and getting yelled at by the guy's team. Scottie made every clue vulgar, and Jay even got into the game. By the time the game was over, the girls had won by a landslide. They moved onto a quieter game as Em could see Jay was starting to fatigue.

She opened Scattergories and passed out the folders to write their answers in then asked if anyone needed any refills before she sat down. Jay's co-worker, Ronak, rolled the die. It landed on the letter S. He pressed the timer to begin the round. Everyone put their heads down and began writing. There was a list of clues, and the object of the game was to come up with words which start with the letter rolled to answer the clue.

When the time buzzed, everyone looked up and closed their folders except Jay. Emmaline watched his face. He didn't seem frustrated, he seemed angry. An emotion he rarely showed. He was usually calm in all situations. She uncrossed her legs and got up out of her chair. She walked over and stood behind him. She noticed his answer sheet was empty except for the letter S going down the row. "I can't think of anything. My mind is completely blank," he said in a harsh tone. She could see he was visibly upset with himself.

"Babe, it's okay. It's hard to think when you're put on the spot. It happens to all of us."

"No, you don't understand." He grabbed at the hair at the front of his head. "It's there. I know it's there. I just can't grasp it." Emmaline stood behind him and wrapped her arms around his shoulders to comfort him, hugging him from behind. He stood up quickly hitting her chin with the back of his head and throwing her arms off of himself. "Stop babying me. I don't need you being all Nurse Em on me. Can't you leave me alone." Jay stomped up the stairs and down the hall to their room. Emmaline tried to recover from the blow and shock of his words. The room became eerily silent.

"Em," Josie began to speak quietly, sadness in her voice.

"It's okay, Josie. I'm fine. Maybe this was too much. I think we should call it a night. Thank you all for coming over." The six friends stood up. They began cleaning up the room. "Don't worry about it. I'll take care of it later." They all quietly said their goodbyes, hugging her on their way out the door.

Josie stayed behind for a few extra moments. "Are you okay?"

"I don't know what to do for him. He hasn't made an appointment to start therapy. He's getting harder and harder to be around. He's always agitated by something. Something I do, something I say, something he can't do. I miss the old Jay. This new Jay... sometimes it's like I'm living with a stranger. I miss the man I married."

Josie walked over to her friend. "Em, you've been around enough patients to know who they are after a brain injury is who they are. They can adjust, adapt, but they are never going to be who they once were. You're going to have to stop comparing new Jay to old Jay. You're going to have to accept him for who he is now. Love him for where he is now. He may be different in some ways, but he is still *your* Jay."

"I'm scared," her lip quivered as she spoke.

"I know. He'll get there. It's going to take time, but he will reach a point of acceptance and be ready to start healing. Do you remember what you both said to each other on your wedding day? 'From this day forward, for better or worse, I promise my heart to you.' You need to reflect on those words. My friend, you are strong. You both are. You will get through this. We are all here for you." Josie pulled Em into a hug and then turned and left.

Emmaline started cleaning up from the night, but Josie's words had struck her hard. Old Jay, new Jay. He was Jay and he was her home. Although they had only been together for a couple of years before they got married, she felt like they were waiting for their paths to finally cross so they could be together forever. She remembered his proposal and their wedding day like they happened last week. Her heart filled with warmth and love at the memory.

It was the middle of the night; they had gone out for a late dinner and came home for dessert in bed. Their lovemaking lasted for what seemed like hours of soft kisses, sweaty bodies, and impassioned eyes gazing at each other. Jay had gazed down at Emmaline lying next to him. He told her she was the most beautiful thing he had ever seen. Their bodies naturally melted together during their lovemaking. Everything about them together felt so right to her. He glanced over her petite body lying comfortably in the bed. Normally, she would be uncomfortable having someone gaze at her this way. With Jay, everything felt natural. She decided she never wanted to leave that spot. She wanted him by her side forever.

He reached over and brushed a lock of her shoulder-length brown hair off her face. "Marry me."

"What?" Em turned her head toward him to make sure she heard him correctly.

"I mean it. Emmaline Jacobs, I want to spend the rest of my life with you. Will you marry me?" He took her delicate hands in his, gently drawing them to his lips, kissing each finger.

His eyes met hers with an expression she couldn't figure out. It was a mix of fear, apprehension, and excitement. Emmaline slowly sat up, supporting her back on the Shaker headboard. "Jay, I..." she began.

"The past two years have been the best of my life. I know I want a lifetime with you. We both had difficult moments in our lives because of what happened with our fathers. We are both strong on our own and stronger together. I know we can face anything if we have each other. Life will be different for our family. I will never do to you what our fathers did to our mothers. I am not that guy. Together, we will have the life we had wished for ourselves. Here in our log cabin, we'll raise our family with love. Our love. For each other, for our children. Em, you are it for me. My heart, my love, my future. Please, say you'll marry me." Jay gazed into her deep, brown eyes. They were brimming with tears of anticipation and nerves.

She sat up a little more, holding his hands tightly. Her heart was pumping fast, she could hear it in her ears as he waited for her answer.

"Yes," she said confidently.

"Really?" He jumped up on the mattress and danced around, making the bed squeak as loud as they had during lovemaking. Emmaline was looking up at him laughing.

"We let go of all the crap from our past, Em. From this day forward, we start a new life, our life...together."

"For better or worse?" she asked, staring up at him with a teasing smile.

"From this day forward, for better or worse. You are mine and I am yours. We can face anything together."

"Okay." She let out a long exhale.

Jay had dropped to his knees and pulled her into him. As they made eye contact, he drew her in for the softest, most loving kiss. "I love you," he said. She started to say it back, but his lips gently pressed onto hers before she could finish. As she pulled away, he met her eyes once again. "From this day forward, for better or worse, Emmaline Jacobs, I promise my heart to you."

Three days later, he surprised her with a wedding at Fenway Park in Boston.

Emmaline had never been to a Boston Red Sox game. She had never even been to Boston. Even though the city was only two hours away, she had never made the trip to Beantown. They had officially been engaged for three days, and Jay had gotten tickets to Sunday's afternoon game for them to celebrate with their best friends. She loved how spontaneous he could be. How full of life he was all the time.

Emmaline jumped in the shower and afterwards threw her Red Sox jersey on that Jay had bought for her the previous day. She could hear voices downstairs. Scottie and Josie must have arrived. She galloped down the stairs only to stop short at the second to last step. Josie was there holding a bouquet of flowers, Scottie had a Red Sox hat with a veil coming out of the top, and Jay was down on one knee with an open ring box in his hand.

"Good morning, beautiful. Will you marry me today?" She slowly stepped down the last two stairs. She moved her gaze from Josie to Scottie and finally met Jay's eyes. She glanced down at the open ring box. The most beautiful matching gold wedding bands were side by side. Realization hit her.

"I'm getting married today," she said it as more of a statement, than a question.

"Yes, you are," Josie replied smiling at her friend.

Jay jumped up from the floor and scooped Emmaline up into his arms. "Yes, we are." Emmaline squealed with excitement while everyone else laughed.

"Come on," Scottie said. "We've got a wedding to get to."

"Wait," Emmaline looked around at all of them. "I have so many questions. Where are we getting married? Who is performing the ceremony? Are we still going to the game? I really want to go to the game. What about my mom? Aunt Viv? Do I need a dress?" Emmaline kept sputtering question after question as her soon-to-be husband and their closest friends led her out of the front door with Jake jumping at their heels. She bent down and kissed their dog on the top of his head, while scratching behind his ears. "Next time I see you, buddy. I will be your mommy officially."

Two and half hours later, they arrived at Fenway Park. Emmaline still did not know what was happening and she didn't care. She was enjoying the day, her wedding day. Jay held her hand as they walked down Jersey Street. She had the baseball hat with a veil on her head and the bouquet of white daisies, her favorite, in her other hand. As they approached the spot with the championship banners, Emmaline saw her mother and aunt standing between the 1903 and 1904 banners. She released Jay's hand and ran into the arms of the two most important women in her life. All her favorite people were there for her special day.

"I can't believe you're here."

"Do you really think we would miss this?" Aunt Viv asked. "Dottie didn't have to ask me twice when she came to pick me up. We busted right out of there."

"I'm so happy for you both," Dottie said through tears, pulling Em into a hug. Viv wrapped her arms around both of them joining in on the moment.

"Okay," Scottie's voice bellowed over everyone. "Let's get this ceremony started. I didn't become an ordained minister yesterday for nothing."

The group laughed as Jay took Emmaline's hand. They both turned and faced Scottie. He pulled a folded sheet of paper from his pocket. Everyone laughed as he unfolded his wedding script and began, "Family and friends, we are gathered here today to bear witness to the joining in marriage of these two people..." A small crowd gathered around to watch the ceremony. Ten minutes later, Emmaline and Jay sealed their union with a passionate kiss. Cheers and clapping came from the small crowd around them. Josie took pictures of it all on her cell phone.

Jay scooped Emmaline up in his arms and carried her across the threshold of the stadium's entrance. Emmaline whispered into his ear, "from this day forward, for better or worse, Jay Ellis, I promise my heart to you." And Emmaline knew she would love him for the rest of her life.

⁓

Emmaline finished cleaning up the kitchen and slowly walked up the stairs to their room. Her heart was heavy. As she walked into their bedroom, she heard a quiet cry. She walked over to the edge of the bed where Jay was lying under the covers. "I don't want to be like this," he said in the saddest voice.

"I know," she sat down next to him on the bed and wrapped her arms around him the best she could. Her heart was breaking for him. "It will get better." She slowly crawled into bed with him as he moved over. They made love that night. Not a hungry love like the night of their engagement, but a soft, quiet, sad love. One to remind themselves they were still connected to each other. Afterward, Jay fell asleep in her arms. She cradled her husband and let the tears she had been holding in gently fall. *From this day forward, for better or worse, we will get through this.* She fell asleep resting her head gently on his.

CHAPTER THIRTEEN

Emmaline

The following weeks were getting harder and harder for Emmaline. It was difficult for her to watch Jay struggling with the mental pain from the headaches. His cognitive function was declining because of his migraines, she tried to talk to him about it, but he became angry with her. She brought up medication once, but it did not go well. "Do you want me to turn into an addict like my father? Is that what you want?" he erupted before charging up to their bedroom and slamming the door.

They were not a couple who had ever fought, but her patience was starting to wane with his irritability every night after work. She didn't know what was happening while he was on the job. She knew he came home each day annoyed with himself and taking his frustrations out verbally on her and Jake. He didn't have the patience to throw the ball for Jake anymore or the physical ability to take him out on the trail as he struggled on the uneven ground. By days end she could tell he was in a lot of pain. He used to have dinner ready for her when she got home from work. They would sit and chat about their day while eating and having a beer or glass of wine. Now he didn't have the energy after his own workday to do any of those things. Because she got home later than he did, most nights they ate soup, sandwiches, or pasta. Emmaline never said anything to him; she took all his silences and outbursts. She tried to make small talk with him about their day, most of the time it was only her talking to him and telling him about her patients at work and Viv's daily antics.

They were spending less and less time with their friends. They tried to do game night a few more times at their house. The last time they all got together, Jay wasn't even participating in the games. He sat off to the side and watched everyone else play. He was making the situation awkward. Nothing anyone did could break him out of his funk. Emmaline knew he had the contact information for the rehab center from Dr. Jim in his bedside table drawer. She saw it there when she was cleaning their room and had to put something away in it. She felt like the business card was calling her from inside the drawer. She wanted to make an appointment for him. With his temper being so unpredictable, she didn't want to take a chance of making him angry. Growing up with a mentally ill and abusive father, there was still an underlying fear that at any moment a man would snap and hit her. She never thought Jay would be that kind of man, but now she didn't know.

Emmaline felt herself getting burnt out from the stress of worrying about him, work and trying to keep life as normal as possible. She was tired all the time, spent most of her days nauseous with worry and she barely had an appetite. She debated about taking a leave of absence from work to help Jay get into his rehab program, but work was her escape from the cloud of despair hanging over their cabin.

"I'm worried about you," Josie said to her over lunch one day. They were eating in the courtyard, soaking up some vitamin D during their lunch break. "You're pale, you're losing weight, you barely eat. You don't look good."

"Gee, thanks, Josie. You're making me feel so much better." Emmaline picked at the crust around the corners of her turkey sandwich.

"I don't know what is really going on with you and Jay, but I do know you can't take care of him if you're not taking care of yourself. Is he still refusing to make the appointment at The Hospital for Special Care?"

"I don't even bring it up anymore. Every time I suggest we go and see what kind of treatment plan they recommend he snaps at me. 'I can handle it, Em. Drop it, Em. I'm not going there so they can drug me up.' I hate seeing him suffer. On Saturday, I watched him walk the lawn mower out of the shed, start it up, and immediately turn it off and put it back. Later in the day, I went out to mow the lawn myself. He got so mad at me. He yelled out of our bedroom window at me to put the mower back. He accused me of thinking he wasn't capable of mowing his own lawn and then said he'd do it another day. Sometimes, it's like I'm married to a stranger. I miss my husband. I miss my Jay. This Jay. I don't know, Josie. He's so different. I don't know how to help him." Emmaline wrapped her sandwich back up in the plastic bag and put it back in her lunchbox. Her appetite was gone.

"I wish I could think of a way to comfort you, but I can't even imagine what you are going through. I'm worried about you, my friend. I don't want you to think Jay's TBI means you have to give up on your dreams for your future together or your dream to become a nurse. You can still do all of it. This is a bump in the long road of your life together." Emmaline knew Josie was trying to comfort her. She loved her best friend. She appreciated her being there, listening and sitting by her side whenever she needed it.

Emmaline met Josephina Diaz at the local community college where they were both studying for their associate's degree in nursing. The connection was instantaneous. Emmaline loved how bold and crass Josie was. She took her out of her comfort zone, helped her find her voice and made her laugh uncontrollably. Em was the most loyal and trustworthy friend Josie had ever had. They both got jobs at The Village at River's Edge Nursing Home around the same time and the next thing they wanted to do together was take the state nursing boards to become registered nurses. Becoming a nurse had been a dream of Emmaline's for as long as she could remember. Her Aunt Viv's early onset dementia diagnosis confirmed for her that she wanted to be a nurse working in elder care.

"I'm not going to give up on Jay or my dream to become a nurse. My hope is Jay will reach a point and accept the help. He needs to let go of the fear that he is going to turn into his father."

"Rip the damn Band-Aid off," a loud voice from behind them said. Josie and Emmaline both jumped.

"Dammit, Viv. Where did you come from?" Josie asked while trying to hold onto the food falling off her lap.

"Listen to me, girly. That boy needs a kick in the ass. No more messing around. You call and get his brain examined. Drag his ass there. Don't even tell him. Your mother wasted too many good years of her life on a deadbeat. You need to know if he's going to be worth your time. It's not you anymore you have to think about." Em stared at her aunt in confusion.

"What are you talking about?" she asked her.

"You got a bun in the oven. You can't be worrying about his ass while taking care of a baby." Viv walked around the front of them and pointed the cane in her hand at Emmaline's belly.

"Viv," Emmaline said with a smile on her face. "I'm not pregnant."

"Hell, you're not. You're sick as a dog, not eating, probably tired all the time. Same as your mama was with you. That handsome hunk of a man may be sick in the head, but his wanker ain't got nothing wrong with it. You're pregnant, girlie." Viv put her cane back down on the ground and walked away from them singing a showtune.

"Holy shit, Em. Are you pregnant?" Josie let the food on her lap drop to the ground.

"What? No? I can't be." Emmaline stopped and thought for a moment. When was the last time she had her period? When was the last time she and Jay had slept together? She felt Josie's shocked eyes on her as the wheels in her head calculated through dates. "I...umm..." Tears began to well up in her eyes. "I don't know." Emmaline scanned the courtyard around them with her eyes like she was searching for an answer or an escape from her current situation. "Oh my god, Josie. What if I'm pregnant? The last time Jay and I had sex was the first night we hosted trivia at the cabin which was six or seven weeks ago."

"Have you missed a period?"

"I can't remember. Maybe, I guess. I mean, Jay wore condoms. The last time sort of happened. We were in a moment. Not a hot and heavy moment. It was a sad let's find comfort in each other moment. Josie, what if I'm pregnant?" Emmaline turned in shock and disbelief making eye contact with her friend. Tears began to fall on her cheeks. "Oh my god, Josie. I can't be pregnant. It's not the right time." Emmaline covered her face with both of her hands trying to hide her silent tears. "We wanted to start a family, but we can't right now. This is all wrong. This is not how we wanted it to be." She spoke softly while shaking her head side-to-side.

"Well, only one way to find out. Guess we are heading to the pharmacy after work today." Josie leaned down to pick up Emmaline's food remnants off the ground and then headed back into work. Emmaline sat there on the bench in silence. Was it possible? Could she be pregnant? She and Jay had talked about starting a family together sooner than later, but not this soon. Not with everything else going on in their lives right now. They needed to take care of him before they could take care of a baby. It wasn't the right time for her to be pregnant. A wave of fear overcame her. She had wanted to be a mother as much as she wanted to be a nurse. Before she let her mind get too far ahead of her, she had to take a test first to confirm what her aunt thought, but in her heart, she felt it. She was pregnant.

CHAPTER FOURTEEN

Emmaline

People talk, especially when your husband is a police officer. Especially when your husband was a police officer who was also involved in a car accident where a young girl died. Emmaline didn't want to take a chance. She was too nervous to buy the pregnancy test herself. After work, Josie drove to CVS and bought the test for her. Emmaline sat in her car outside Josie's apartment building. Her hands were shaking as she texted Jay.

Em: Going over to Josie's for a bit after work.

Jay: K

K? The old Jay would have made some sarcastic remark about the two of them staying out of trouble or to have fun or to call him if she needed a ride home. His one letter response made her heart sad.

Emmaline heard tires rolling in behind her on the paved driveway. She peered into her rearview mirror and saw Josie's old gold sedan making its way to the spot closest to her car. She slowly dropped her phone into her bag and turned off the black Jeep. As she climbed out of her vehicle, she saw Josie walking over to her with two test kits, one in each hand.

"Oh my god, Josie, you could have at least put those in a bag."

"What? No one is here. No one will see them and if they do, they'll think they are mine."

Emmaline rolled her eyes at her friend. "Can we please go inside? I want to get this over with. My heart is in my throat, and I can't stop shaking. I need to know." Emmaline followed Josie to the front door of the blue apartment building. She lived in a complex where each building had four apartments, two on the left, two on the right, one apartment over the other. Josie lived upstairs on the left. She slowly opened the storm door holding it open with her hip while she unlocked the front door. To Emmaline the world was moving in slow motion.

She followed Josie up the stairs and to the left. While she waited for Josie to unlock the door to her apartment, Emmaline kept repeating to herself internally, *please, don't be pregnant, please don't be pregnant.* Once inside the apartment, Em grabbed the tests from Josie's hand and raced down the hall to the bathroom. The smell of lavender and coconut enveloped her as she closed the door. She had to lean her head against the back of the door to catch her breath. From the other side she heard, "Em, everything is going to be fine. I'm here if you need me. I'll even hold the stick for you to pee on." Em smiled to herself. In this moment, she was grateful for her friend.

She slowly opened one of the boxes, unwrapped the instructions and laid them out on the counter. "I'm scared," she said in a whisper.

"Em, can I come in?" Emmaline didn't realize Josie was standing on the other side of the door. She turned the knob to let her friend into the bathroom. Streams of tears ran down her face as Josie walked into the room. "I got you, babe." Josie picked up the directions and began reading through them. "Go ahead and sit on the toilet."

Emmaline sat down on the top of the toilet seat with her pants still on. Josie laughed at her. "No. You have to pull your pants down and sit on the toilet. Unless you plan on peeing through your scrubs."

Em stood up and lifted the toilet seat, pulled down her pants, and sat back down. "I don't know, Josie. I've never done this before."

Josie pulled off the removable cap of the test to reveal the applicator and handed the stick to Emmaline. "Here, pee on this end." Emmaline took it from her and stuck it between her legs.

"Well, don't look at me. I can't pee while you are looking at me."

"Sorry." Josie laughed, turning her head the other away. "This is how much I love you. I will even hold your pee stick while we wait for the timer." She pulled her phone out of her pocket and set the timer on her phone for five minutes. Em handed her the pregnancy test while she cleaned herself up. They did not have to wait for the timer to go off. Two lines appeared almost instantly, the colors like a neon sign in Times Square flashing, *You're Pregnant*. They both stared at it.

"Oh my god, oh my god, oh my god." Em flung the bathroom door open and began pacing across Josie's apartment. "I can't be pregnant now. This is not how it was supposed to happen. This is not what we planned. We were going to have fun trying. I was going to wrap the positive pregnancy test in a gift box and surprise him with it. He was going to pick me up and spin me around with excitement. This is not how starting our family was supposed to be."

Emmaline walked around the small dining room/living room combination muttering to herself. Josie stood there and let her friend verbally process the news before she spoke. "Hey, this could be a good thing," Josie cautiously said. "Maybe the news of a pregnancy will snap Jay out of his funk. Maybe he'll finally call and make the appointment with the doctor's office." Em knew Josie was trying to be encouraging as she watched her continue to pace the room, twisting her hands together over and over.

"What if he doesn't? What if he keeps getting worse and I have to take care of him *and* a baby? What if his anger and irritability turn violent? I don't want that for my child. I will not let my child grow up in an abusive house like I did. We've only been married for one year. The plans we made for our future together, they're gone. I know it sounds selfish of me, but I'm sad, and I'm mad. What I thought would be my future has changed, and I didn't have a say in any of it. We got married, I was going to pass my boards and get an RN position, we were going to start a family. We had a plan. What's happening right now, I don't want any of it." Emmaline was voicing her inner fears. Thoughts she wasn't sure she was ready to say aloud but just came pouring out. She knew Josie was one of the few people she could say these things to.

"Okay, Em, you of all people know plans can change. I'm sure your mom didn't go into her marriage thinking her husband was going to be an abusive asshole who was mentally unstable. She kicked him out, finished raising you on her own. You turned out amazing. Your mom is also a fabulous baker who makes the best damn soda bread I've ever tasted."

"What are you saying? Do you think I should leave Jay now because I'm going to eventually be raising this kid on my own anyway?" Em thought of the day her mom finally threw her dad out of the house. She knew now her father had an undiagnosed mental illness, but at the time, they lived in constant fear of his mood shifts, his outbursts. They would be sitting at the kitchen table eating dinner, laughing one minute and then the next he would pick up his plate of food and throw it across the room and follow it up with a backhand to her mother or herself. Then later he would cry to both of them apologizing for his behavior, declaring his love for them.

She was so proud of her mother the day she had the locks of the house changed and left her father's belongings in a suitcase on the front step. She was twelve years old at the time. The strange thing was he didn't even fight it. They were hiding inside the house when he came home Wednesday after work. She and her mom both had bruises on their arms and faces from his tirade the night before. Her school had called the Department of Children and Family Services after they finally got Emmaline to admit what happened to her. After spending most of the afternoon talking to a caseworker and police officer, Dottie walked up the stairs and packed all her husband's clothes and toiletries into one large suitcase. Dottie placed the suitcase outside, then walked back into the house, closed the door, and locked it. The sound of the door clicking shut and the lock turning represented them closing the door to the life they knew and turning a new chapter. Mother and daughter together, no more fear. When her dad got home from work, she watched him exit his car and stare at the suitcase. Then he slowly walked up to the front of the house, picked up his suitcase and left. He drove away that day and Emmaline did not see him again.

"Em, I'm not saying you should leave Jay. I'm saying you can't predict what life is going to bring. Your parents were a bad example. I think you need to give Jay the benefit of the doubt. He's not your dad. He's a really good guy going through a really hard time. You guys planned your life to go in one direction. Now it's going in another direction. Neither one is better than the other, it's just different. You are both amazing people. Give him time."

Em was not in the state of mind to process Josie's words. She needed time to think. She grabbed her keys off the kitchen table and the unopened pregnancy test kit. She hugged her friend. "I love you."

"Love you too," Josie said, returning the hug.

That night after Jay had fallen asleep, she quietly took one of the tests from the box and tried it again. Still positive. The next morning, before Jay woke up, she took the other one. Still pregnant. She knew she was going to have to tell him. She didn't know how or when. Being around him lately felt like walking on eggshells. It was the same feeling she used to have with her father. She needed time to think, to figure out what her next steps would be. What she really wanted was for Jay to get help. Maybe if her father had, their lives would have been different. She didn't know how to convince Jay to make the call. She leaned against the bathroom wall staring down at the positive pregnancy test in her hand. She made an unspoken promise to the baby growing inside her that she would never let anyone hurt them. Until she knew what to do, she would go on with life as usual.

CHAPTER FIFTEEN

Jay

Thanksgiving came and went without any fanfare. Jay and Emmaline had dinner at Dottie's house, as it was the family tradition. He felt like all eyes were on him. The other guests made small talk with him, but mostly he felt their pity. While Em helped Dottie do the dishes afterwards he put the card table and folding chairs back down in the basement. They left right after, not staying for after dinner drinks. Emmaline put it on herself saying she was tired, and they were going to head home. Jay hated it when she made excuses for them. He felt everyone knew it was because of him and not her.

As soon as they got home, Jay went straight to bed. All the sounds, lights, and noise had brought on another headache. There was too much stimulation all day and he needed quiet. Em didn't say anything other than goodnight before he went up the stairs with a gentle kiss on the lips. He wished he could do better for her. He didn't have it in him.

The next morning, Jay awoke to the sun peeking through the slats in the blinds. "Jay, I'm heading out for my run. You better get up or you'll be late for work again." Jay heard Emmaline's voice from down the hall. He was tired all the time. Each day he struggled more to wake up. Since the accident, he had been experiencing mental fog, physical fatigue, and restless sleep, but now he was sleeping even more. Pino had texted him a few times after work about going to the driving range. The first time, Jay had told him he was too tired. The next few messages, he didn't even bother to text back. He didn't have the energy to do anything after work. He wanted to sleep.

His workdays were getting harder as well. He kept forgetting different pieces of equipment for roll call in the morning. He was struggling to draft his end-of-day reports. He couldn't recall all the details about things that happened in the day. Lieutenant Bonetti had pulled him aside a couple of times to point out the discrepancies. Jay was embarrassed. Since joining the force, he had been at the top of his game. He had never been spoken to by a superior about deficiencies in his work.

He was the guy who said hello to everyone in the station when he got there in the morning and goodbye to everyone when he left at the end of the day. Now he would try to sneak in unnoticed or stare down at his phone as he walked by his colleagues. He couldn't stand to see the looks of pity for him on their faces. He knew his TBI was affecting his job performance as well. The sound of the siren was too much for his headaches, so he pretended not to see the speeding cars. He would park his car and lean on the front of it with his radar gun so the cars would slow down the minute they saw him there.

He was so annoyed with himself by the end of each day he began taking his frustrations out verbally on Emmaline and Jake. He didn't have the strength to throw the ball for Jake or physical ability to take him on the trail for a walk. By days end his head was throbbing like a heartbeat behind his left eye. He used to have dinner ready for Em when she got home from work, now he didn't have the energy after his own workday to cook anymore. Emmaline never said anything to him; she took all his silence and outbursts. She tried to make small talk with him about their days. He sat with his head down eating his dinner with an occasional "Oh" or "Uh huh."

He was struggling. He still had Dr. Jim's business card with his cell phone number written on the back. He had stashed it in his bedside table when he had gotten home from the hospital. He felt like the rectangle piece of cardstock was calling to him from inside the drawer. Whenever Em brought up making the appointment he would snap at her telling her he could handle it on his own. She was supportive, but he could sense her skepticism when she saw him struggling to recall information. He tried to hide his migraines but even hiding them was getting harder and harder as their intensity increased by days end.

On Friday when Jay pulled into his driveway, he saw Pino's truck sitting at the end. Jay was trying to recall if they had made plans for after work. He parked his truck in its usual spot then got out. As he came around to the other side Pino met in the middle of the gravel drive.

"Hey, did we have plans for today?"

"No, I wanted to come over and see you. I haven't seen you in a while and I needed to check up on you. Thought maybe you and I could go grab a beer together." Scottie had his hands in his jeans pockets and was rocking back and forth on his heels.

"I'm pretty wiped out from the week." Jay saw disappointment in Pino's eyes. "How about we sit out back and have a beer here instead?" Scottie perked up and followed Jay into the house. Jake met them both at the door with his long, black tail wagging. "Help yourself to a beer. Let me go change out of my uniform."

Ten minutes later, the two friends were sitting outside on the cabin's back patio watching Jake run after his tennis ball. "How've you been feeling?" Scottie asked.

"I'm good. Managing." Jay took a swig of his beer.

"Come on, man. I know you better than you know yourself. You are not good, you're hurting. I see it, we all see it. You're the only one who doesn't want to say it out loud."

"Fine, it hasn't been easy. I'm still dealing with headaches from the accident, some brain fog, fatigue, and my balance is a bit off."

"Still against the rehab center?"

"Pino, I don't want to end up hooked on meds like my dad. You remember him before and after so I would expect of all people you would understand. The guy I knew before his accident and the guy afterwards were two different people. I don't want to be like."

Jay's father was a steel worker who was injured on the job. A steel bar detached from a chain and came down on his dad's back. He had multiple surgeries to repair the spinal damage. The operations only did so much for his father. He lived in chronic pain every day. In the end, he became addicted to the pain killers he was prescribed. Jay watched his father change. As the pain got worse, Jay saw his father pop more and more pills throughout the day. His doctor refused to increase the prescription. His father took matters into his own hands and found the pills in other places, mostly on the streets. Then one day, Jay's dad disappeared. About a year later, his mother sat him down and told Jay his father had either committed suicide or accidentally died from an overdose. She explained to him the pain was too much for his father to bear.

"Jay, I'm sorry to say. You're already like that. I'm not saying this to upset you, but you're not the same. You never want to go out anymore, you never return texts or calls. From what the guys at the station tell me, you hardly talk to anyone at work either. You may not realize it, but you're slipping away from everyone, especially Em." Scottie kept his eyes forward as he disclosed all of this to Jay. Each thing his friend mentioned was like a stabbing to his heart.

"Did she say anything to you?"

"She didn't have to. I can see it in her face when I run into her. You are both shells of the people you used to be. You were Jay and Emmaline. The dream couple. I'm sorry for you, man, I really am. What happened totally sucks, but how much longer can you go on like this? I know this is not the life you both wanted together. Remember, I was there the day you got married. Hell, I officiated the wedding."

Jay knew his friend was right. He didn't know where to start. He felt like he was living in someone else's body, someone else's mind. He didn't recognize himself.

"Tomorrow afternoon, a few of us are going to the new indoor golf range. You guys should come. We are going around three thirty. JD and Stacy were able to get a sitter for their kids for the afternoon." Scottie stood up and drained the rest of his beer. "Even for an hour, come and hang out, it will be good for you. For both of you." Scottie patted Jay on the back of his shoulder as he made his way back into the house. Jay sat in silence as he listened to his friend's truck rev up and pull out of the driveway.

Maybe he's right. Maybe an afternoon out was what he and Em needed to help them reconnect to the fun couple they once were.

CHAPTER SIXTEEN

Jay

Emmaline was surprised when Jay suggested the outing with their friends. He knew she wasn't into golf, but an afternoon with their group of friends was exactly what they needed. They had a fun time. It was the most relaxed he had been since the accident. He had finally started to feel a bit like himself. The afternoon with friends kickstarted him into wanting to get out of bed more. The next morning, he took Jake for a walk in the woods and continued it each day before and after work. He also had dinner ready when Em got home from work. On Wednesday night, he tried staying up long enough to snuggle up on the couch with her to watch a show. Jay went to bed earlier than Emmaline, but he would at least watch one show with her before calling it a night.

She was sitting next to him with her feet tucked under her staring at the screen. They were finally getting around to watching a show everyone said they must see. "You're so far away. Come closer." Em turned to him surprised, then she scooched up next to him and he put an arm around her. She tucked her head into the crook of his shoulder. Jay took a deep inhale of her lavender and mint scented hair. She felt and smelled like home to him. Wrapped in his arms, this is how he wanted them to stay. It had been a long time since he had any kind of sexual urge. She looked up at him, and he realized she had caught him staring at her.

"What?" she asked with a half-smile.

"I love you." He couldn't remember the last time he said those three words to her.

"I love you too." Jay leaned down and placed a gentle kiss on her lips. He kissed her like she was a precious, porcelain doll he did not want to break. Their small kisses increased into a longing he had forgotten in himself. This was his wife, the woman he loved the woman he wanted to have a family with, grow old with. "I've missed you."

He stared into Emmaline's eyes and saw her holding back tears. "I've missed you too," she said. He pulled the throw blanket off of the back of the couch, moved the coffee table out of the way, and with the TV muted in the background and Jake laying down in his dog bed, they made love like two people who had been apart from one another for months. Because that was exactly how he felt.

The next morning Jay stopped at Perino's Bakery on the way to work. He was walking with a lighter step as he made his way from his truck to the bakery's front entrance. As he opened the door the bell hanging from the top jingled. "Well, appears someone is in a good mood." He heard a voice from behind. Jay turned around to see Dottie carrying a box overflowing with bread. Scottie was behind her with two more boxes stacked one on top of the other. "Hold the door. I've got a few more boxes in the car." Jay held the door for them and then walked to Dottie's car to get the last of the boxes.

"Miserable weather we are getting," Dottie said to him as she held the door for him. It was an overcast day, gray and cloudy, perfect weather to keep his headache away, he hoped. It had been that way all week and, oddly enough, he was feeling better because of it.

"I actually kind of like," he told her. The smell of fresh baked bread wafted up from the box to his nose making his stomach grumble. He couldn't remember if he ate breakfast or not. That was also a problem for him. He would forget to eat or think he ate but had not. "Mind if I buy one of these loaves before they are put out on display. I'd love to bring one home to Em."

"Of course. You look good today, Jay. How are you feeling?" Jay had gotten so sick of people asking him how he was feeling. The people at work or out in the community but coming from Dottie was different. There was something about Dottie. He knew he could speak the truth and not just say *fine, good,* or *okay.*

"This week is the first one in a long time I'm actually doing a bit better. It's been a long few months."

"I'm so happy to hear that. And how is your rehab going?" Jay stared down at his feet and then back up at his mother-in-law.

"I'm fine. I don't need it, Dottie. Everything is working itself out. The headaches have subsided, I'm not sleeping as much, and I'm sure I'll be back to running in no time." He knew he was exaggerating a bit for her sake, and he could see in her skeptical glance at him she knew it as well.

"Jay, a traumatic brain injury doesn't go away. Your symptoms are going to ebb and flow. You need to make an appointment. If not for you, then for you and Em. You're not the only one who's been going through this recovery. If you don't want to go by yourself, I'll go with you."

At that moment, Scottie came out of the bakery taking a bite out of a croissant. "Fancy running into you here. Grabbing a goodie before work?" he asked Jay with a mouth full of the pastry.

Dottie scowled at him. "Don't talk with food in your mouth." She harrumphed. "I was telling Jay how good he looks and how I would take him to his rehab appointment if he made one."

"What? You haven't gone yet. Dude, rehab is like physical therapy for your brain. You need to do it. Admitting you need help doesn't make you weak, it shows you're a strong person by listening to what your body needs." Jay knew Scottie was well aware he hadn't made an appointment yet. He was trying to get him in trouble with Dottie. Same shit he used to do to him when they were kids with his own mother.

"Wise words from the boy who used to pick his nose and wipe his boogers on my bread so I couldn't sell it, and he could eat it," Dottie teased. They had a long history together. Scottie was a troublemaker when he was younger, and Dottie liked to remind him of it.

While they bantered back and forth anxiety swelled in Jay. Emmaline had been dropping hints about making the appointment as well. He couldn't pinpoint exactly why, but something kept holding him back. He knew he didn't want drugs because he didn't want to end up like his dad. Overdosed, found on the side of the road. Pino was right, the thought of going to rehab made him feel weak like he couldn't take care of himself, which was something he had been doing since his dad left. Even the word rehab made his heart race in panic.

"I have to get to work. I'll see you all later." Jay turned without making eye contact with either of them. He could sense their eyes on him as he got into his truck and drove away. A feeling of failure washed over him. He'd been so strong, able to take care of himself, these past couple of months since the accident had changed everything. *Why should I get better when Cecelia was dead?* The thought emerged to the forefront of his mind. *Was that why? Do I have survivor's guilt? It was an accident. A tragic accident. Do I need to keep suffering to make up for the fact she is no longer here?*

Later that afternoon as Jay was finishing up his report from the day, Lieutenant Bonetti walked over to his desk. Brian tapped two fingers on the desk while saying, "Jay, come take a walk with me." Jay searched his commanding officer's face. He could not get a read on him from his expression. He stood up and followed the husky man out of the two sets of double doors and into the crisp, early December air.

"Everything okay, sir." Jay was tall standing at five feet eleven inches, but Lieutenant Brian Bonetti towered over him by a full head. The older man looked down at him with concern in his brown eyes.

"Jay, I know since the accident you've been trying to continue on with life as usual. I'm sure it hasn't been easy for you with that young girl passing and then finding out about your own injury. I talked to the chief and sergeant, and we all agree it might be best for you to take some time off. You were injured on the job, and you are owed some medical leave to take care of yourself."

Jay's heart dropped into his stomach. "I'm good, sir, really. I take Advil for the headaches when I need it and I'm getting stronger each day."

Lieutenant Bonetti rubbed a hand over his short, curly black hair. "You're not hearing me, son. We're not asking you. We are telling you. You need to take some time off. Besides forgetting little things each day at roll call, I've found errors in your daily reports. Minor errors, but errors we can't afford to have. You've been snapping at people and overall, you're not yourself. I haven't said anything and maybe I should have said something sooner. We all think it would be best if you took some time off to take care of yourself. The holidays are coming up; it's a good time for an extended holiday leave. Do your treatment plan. Meet with your therapists. I know you haven't gone yet. I speak from experience, taking time to rest, to heal does not make you weak. You need to do this for yourself, for your job, for Emmaline. We are here for you if you need us."

    The lieutenant patted him on the back and then turned back toward the station doors. Jay stood there in shock. He was being forced out on medical leave. Who was he if not a police officer? What was he expected to do with his time? Jay didn't know what to do with himself in that moment. Thoughts were pinging around in his head. He walked back into the station and to the locker room to gather up his belongings. His colleagues' eyes were on him as he was leaving, but he didn't stop to talk to anyone or make eye contact. He walked out to his truck and drove away.

CHAPTER SEVENTEEN

Emmaline

Emmaline was nervous driving home from work. Brian had called her after Jay had left work to fill her in on their decision to put him on medical leave. He told her he was hoping it would be the push Jay needed to finally get treatment. Jay had been doing so well lately. Ever since their outing at the indoor golf range, he seemed happier, more like himself. She was worried this would be a setback for him. She put her blinker on to turn down their street. Nervous anticipation rose in her as she drove closer to their home. As she pulled into their driveway, she noticed the outside lights were off and there was only one light on in their living room. It got dark earlier now. Seven thirty felt more like nine o'clock. Their long driveway and yard were pitch black. The glow of her headlights illuminated the house as she pulled in next to Jay's truck.

Emmaline took her time gathering her lunchbox and purse. She walked toward the cabin with slow apprehension, not knowing what she was walking into. She was reluctant to open the front door. When she finally did, Jake came running over to her from his dog bed in front of the fireplace.

"Hey boy," she whispered while scratching him behind his ears. "How ya doing?" She walked over to the kitchen island placing her lunchbox down and then over to the back door letting Jake out to do his business. She didn't know if she should yell up to Jay like she didn't know what happened earlier. Let him tell her and act surprised or let him know Brian had called her with the news. She decided on the latter. No reason to tiptoe around it. Being a police officer was a part of Jay's whole being. It wasn't simply what he did, it was who he was. She knew how hard this was going to be for him.

After letting Jake back inside, she gave him his biscuit and headed up the stairs. She stopped at the door to their bedroom, taking a deep breath before walking into the dark room. "Hey babe." Jay was lying face down on the bed still in his uniform. The placement of his body told her he felt defeated.

"I was let go today," he mumbled from the side of the pillow.

"Brian called me. That may be how you perceive it, but in your heart, you know it's a leave and not a let go."

Jay rolled over onto his back, propping an arm under his head. "What do I do now, Em. I'm a police officer. Who am I if not an officer? What am I supposed to do with myself now?"

Emmaline could physically see his heart sunk in his chest with the weight of all of this. "Well, you'll have time to decorate the cabin for Christmas now," she tried to joke but it fell flat. "How about taking these next few weeks off as more of an extended holiday vacation. Focus on building your strength, spend more time with me," she teased. "Maybe go visit your mom in Florida. Change of scenery?"

She was trying to be encouraging. It wasn't working "Why did this have to happen now? I was finally doing better. Like my old self." He moved the arm from behind his head and put it over his eyes.

"Take a few more minutes for yourself. I'm going to go

downstairs and make us some dinner and then we can continue watching our show together." She rose from the bed and left the room. She had no idea what she could do to help comfort him.

─────※─────

Jay didn't come down for dinner. He fell asleep. In fact, he spent most of the week in bed or on the couch watching mindless television. Actually, the TV was on, but she didn't know if he was really watching it. He stayed in pajamas or sweats all day. He didn't leave the house. Before Em left for work, she would encourage him to go out for a walk with Jake. When she came home and asked if he did, he would tell her it was too cold out. If this is what depression was like, Jay was in it. He was snapping at Em again and avoiding calls and texts from friends. Scottie stopped by to see him one day, and Jay had sent him away claiming he had a migraine. Em walked Scottie out to his truck asking him if he had any ideas for ways she could help Jay. Unfortunately, he didn't have any.

He looked at her and said, "You can't help him if he doesn't want to help himself." She knew Scottie was right.

In group text with their friends, messages were going around about making plans for the holiday trivia night at Mountain Laurel Brewing. The brewery was having an ugly sweater contest as part of the last trivia night of the year. They were all sharing photos of their ugliest sweaters. She watched Jay glanced down at the text flashing on his phone, but he didn't bother to open the messages. He hadn't told Em and didn't have to. She already knew he would not be going.

─────※─────

After she got out of work the following Tuesday night, Emmaline drove over to the cabin to pick Jay up for trivia night. She had texted him in the afternoon to tell him she would be there. Even though they hadn't spoken much about the night, she was still holding out hope he would go. He needed to get out of the house. She texted him every day while she was at work. She mostly got one-word answers in response. *Fine, good, okay.* When she walked into the cabin all the lights were out. She found him in bed, under the covers. "Jay," she said as she walked over to the bedside table and turned the lamp on.

"Turn it off," he snapped at her. She didn't listen. She moved the blanket down from over his head.

"Jay, it's time for trivia. Time to get up and get ready. I have an ugly sweater you can wear. I borrowed it from Aunt Viv." She laughed awkwardly.

Jay tugged the blanket back over his head. "I'm not going. My head hurts too much. I can't handle the lights and all the noise." He grumbled at her as his arm came out from under the covers and his hand searched for the lamp to turn the light back off. Emmaline was too tired to fight with him. She bent down and kissed his head through the blanket then turned and left the room.

There was a part of her which was disappointed that Jay didn't want to go to trivia night and yet another part of her was a little relieved. She needed a break from him. He was getting harder and harder to be around. When Emmaline met Jay, he was magnetic. She felt a pull toward him like she had never experienced before. As she got to know him more, she realized this was his personality. Jay drew everyone in. His gorgeous smile, welcoming demeanor, and his big personality were captivating. His eyes were the color of chocolate, like the kind of chocolate you find in a chocolate fountain, so smooth, so delicious. You melted right into them. Which is exactly what she did the first night they met at the brewery. When she looked at him now, she saw a shell of the man he once was. His brain injury, the accident had taken part of him away from her, away from their friends. She missed the old Jay.

Driving into the brewery parking lot, she felt a wave of sadness wash over her for even having those thoughts. She knew she needed this night out, yet she felt guilty for wanting the time to herself. When she walked into the brewery, she glanced around and spotted Josie and their group of friends. Josie made eye contact with her. Em shook her head side-to-side confirming Jay had not come with her. Em turned her head, and her eyes met Scottie's. The smile on his face turned downward, and he turned his head back to the friends at his table. She walked over to her table; Josie handed her a Sprite. She was so grateful for her friend's thoughtfulness. Her stomach had felt nauseous all day. She glanced around at everyone as she sat down at the table putting a fake smile on her face for the rest of their group. Josie reached over and squeezed her hand as if to reassure Emmaline that she knew she was hurting and she was there for her.

Trivia night was not full of fun and laughter like usual. As soon as the team totals were tallied and announced, Emmaline said her goodbyes. The nausea had intensified throughout the evening. The itchiness from Viv's sweater was driving her crazy. She was all around miserable. She wanted to get back home, maybe take a bath and crawl into bed.

When she arrived home, the house was pitch black, no lights on inside or outside. Emmaline walked through the house and up the stairs. Jake was inside the bedroom door whining for her. "Hey boy," she said as she slowly opened the door. "I bet you would like to go out." Emmaline walked back down the stairs with Jake and let him out the back door. She heated up a bowl of soup for Jay, figuring he probably hadn't eaten any dinner. The smell of the soup only increased the nauseous building up inside her.

After letting Jake back in and giving him a piece of rawhide, she walked back up the stairs with the soup. She breathed through her mouth to avoid the smell of the chicken noodle soup. The smell of the chicken was making her stomach churn. As she walked over to the bedside table and turned the lamp on, the smell became too much for her. She quickly put the soup down and ran into the bathroom. She barely made it in time to the toilet bowl before vomiting.

"Are you drunk?" Emmaline heard his critical tone while she rested the side of her face on the edge of the toilet. She could sense his presence looming over her. A negative energy radiated from him.

"No. I'm not feeling well." She still hadn't told him she was pregnant. She had been waiting for the right time, but ever since he was put on medical leave there never seemed to be a right time.

She heard him turn and leave, closing the door behind him. The old Jay would have knelt beside her, the old Jay would have pulled her hair back and put it in a hair tie. She wanted her old Jay back. Tears streamed down her face as she got sick again. This was not how it was supposed to be. This was not what they had planned.

After the nausea finally subsided, Emmaline cleaned herself up. She didn't even bother to stop and talk to him. He was back in bed under the covers with the light turned out. Emmaline walked down the stairs. She pulled the navy blue, sherpa throw blanket off the back of the couch and laid down, resting her head on a throw pillow. With the corner of the blanket curled up in her hands silent tears ran down her face.

The pinging of Emmaline's cell phone woke her up the next morning. It took her a second to orient herself remembering she slept on the couch. She reached behind the back of her to the sofa table and grabbed the purse she had placed there the night before. She pulled out her cell phone and saw the text was from her mother. The time flashed six forty-five. Dottie was an early riser thanks to all her years as a baker. Em opened the message and read it.

Dottie: How is he?

Emmaline: Not good.

Dottie: Therapy yet?

Emmaline: Nope. Mom, it's bad. I want him to see Dr. Jim, but he's been so depressed since being put on medical leave I'm afraid to even bring it up. When did you know Viv couldn't take care of herself anymore and you needed to intervene?

Emmaline's phone rang. It was her mother. "Hey."

"Do you remember when I had Viv move in with me after she couldn't live by herself anymore?" Dottie asked.

"Yes."

"About six or seven months after she started getting more confused. She repeated herself, asked the same questions over and over or would think she was supposed to be places she didn't need to be. Remember how mad she got when I wouldn't take her to see the Rockette's for their holiday spectacular at Radio City Music Hall? It was the middle of the summer." Dottie laughed through the phone. A smile formed on Emmaline's face. No matter how disoriented or vulgar her aunt got, she adored her.

"Do you remember the Rogers family who used to live diagonally across the street from us?"

"Yes, of course I do," Emmaline replied not knowing where her mother was going with this conversation.

"Mr. Rogers came over one day and rang the doorbell. When I opened the door, he was standing there with a coffee cake in his hand. It was a perfect spiral coffee cake like the one Viv makes with the nice white, icy frosting and cinnamon sprinkled on top. I asked him how he was doing and if the cake was for us. He told me Vivian had made it for them and brought it over to their house the day before, but they have so much coffee cake they couldn't eat anymore. He said Viv had brought coffee cake over to them the last three days in a row, forgetting she had already brought them one the previous day. She did all this while I was out delivering my bread. It was at that point I knew she needed to be in a place where she would get round the clock care. I knew I wasn't going to be able to help her in the way she needed to be helped. Her dementia had progressed far enough along that I didn't want to risk her walking out the door and not remembering how to get back home. I had already toured River's Edge and knew it's where I wanted her to be. I finally made the call to get her on the list for a room."

"How will I know with Jay?" she quietly whispered into the phone. Jay was asleep upstairs; she didn't want to risk him waking up and overhearing her side of the conversation.

"Oh, believe me, you'll know. Something he will say or do and then you'll feel an invisible tap on the shoulder telling you it's time."

When Jay finally woke up, Emmaline made him get dressed and go to the bakery with her. She needed to get him out of the house.

She knew her mother's fresh baked bread would be a good incentive. He insisted on staying in the Jeep while she went into the store. Scottie's mom came out and dragged him into the bakery. The interaction between Jay, Mrs. Perino and the other customers was uncomfortable for everyone. Jay made no attempt to be friendly or conversational. He stood there while others talked around him. Mrs. Perino loaded them up with more baked goods than either one of them could ever eat. She climbed into the Jeep next to Jay. She glanced over at him. She didn't recognize the man sitting next to her. The husband she once knew didn't exist anymore. On their wedding day, they vowed to each other from this day forward, for better or worse, they would be together through it all. *We were too young and naive to know life doesn't always go as planned.*

CHAPTER EIGHTEEN

Jay

Later that morning, Jay heard a knock, a loud and persistent knock at the door. "We're coming in?" a familiar voice yelled. He pulled his head up from the bed he had climbed back into after Emmaline had left for work. Sets of feet stomped their way up the stairs and down the hall. He looked up to see Dottie and Viv staring at him. "Get up, lazy bones. You're spending the day with us." Viv walked over to him, grabbed his hand, and dragged him out of the bed. Minutes later he was sitting on a bar stool in his own kitchen with the smells of eggs and toast being cooked and the sounds of two old ladies bickering at each other.

"I told you if you get eggs shells in the pan use the shell to scoop it out." Dottie leaned over her sister who was using the pad of her pinkie finger to try and grab the broken shell out of the raw egg in the pan.

"Listen, baby sister, I've been cooking eggs while you were still sucking on Mom's titty. Don't you tell me how to cook." Jay picked up the mug of tea in front of him and brought the cup to his nose to smell it. *Not the same as coffee.*

"Can I ask why you are here? And can I exchange this for

coffee?" He lifted the mug to the two of them. Dottie scuttered around the kitchen, opening and closing cabinets and drawers. He wanted to ask her if she could be a little quieter but didn't know if she would even hear him over Viv singing about putting on the bacon and frying it up in a pan.

"No, you cannot have coffee. Jim said no coffee. It doesn't help your migraines. You're switching to tea. Try it; it's good. We are here to help get your ass out of bed, get over yourself and start getting better. No more wallowing in your own self-pity. You're better than that." Dottie lectured him as she cut up strawberries emphasizing her words by pointing the small knife at him. "I brought this one along because she seemed to be having a lucid day when I stopped by this morning."

"I'm not Lucy. I'm Viv. Jesus Christ, you'd think she'd know her own sister. Lucy was the creepy girl down the street who looked at me like she wanted to fuck me."

"Lucid, not Lucy, you SOB. And you're right, she was gay. She married a really nice woman. They opened the jewelry shop up in Litchfield I take you to sometimes." Dottie pushed a plate of strawberries across the counter to Jay.

"Oh, yeah. I like that place a lot. Hmm...I think they'd both like a turn with me. You know, we old people are still virile." Viv turned to Jay and winked at him.

"Tone it down, Viv," Dottie said placing strawberries on the two other plates in front of her. "So, I have this one broken out of the home until two. You, sir, are going to eat breakfast, take a shower, get dressed, and then spend the day with a couple of sassy old broads. Come on, Jake, time to go out." Jake's ears perked up at the word out. He had been lying on the floor next to Jay. Dottie walked around the counter. She stopped next to Jay, staring him directly in the eyes. "Jay, I know how much you love my daughter, and I know how much she loves you. My husband was a deadbeat from the start. I never should have married him, but at least I got Emmaline out of the marriage. You, though, you are the real deal." She grabbed one of his hands into both of hers. "We're going to help you through this. But no more screwing around being the tough guy. It's time to start taking your recovery seriously and get better. For you *and* your wife."

Tears welled up in Jay's eyes as Dottie let his hand go and walked to the back door with Jake. "She's not wrong. Her ex was a bastard. I told her she never should have married him, but you can't tell someone that infatuated anything. The best thing she ever did was kick his ass to the curb. You know she still keeps track of him to make sure he doesn't come back for her or Em. She even has pictures of herself with all her bruises and casted parts. She told him if he ever came back, she'd take the pictures right to the police. She's a smart woman, that one." Viv scooped eggs onto the three plates on the counter.

"Wow, I had no idea. Does Em know?" Jay took a sip of his tea. It wasn't bad.

"No way. Dottie has never told her. You know you're not going to be them. Her dad, your dad. It's not you, son. You're better than either of them could ever be. Regardless of what's going on in that head of yours, your heart is as good as they come." She pointed the spatula to his forehead and then pointed it down to his chest. Dottie walked back into the house with Jake. She turned her head from one to the other with a questioning stare. "Thank God your back, I had to fight him off with this spatula. I can't help it I ooze sex appeal." Viv turned and put the pan and utensil in the sink.

Dottie and Viv cleaned up from brunch while Jay showered and got dressed. "Hurry it up, Jay. We have to go," Viv yelled up the stairs to him. Jay had no idea how two older women could turn him back into a little boy wanting to please so quickly. He didn't have time to feel sorry for himself that day. They rushed him out the door and into Dottie's olive-green Subaru Forrester.

Jay sat in the back seat with his head scraping the ceiling of the car as he listened to the sister's bicker about everything from the choice of music to which route they should be taking.

Dottie pulled into the driveway of the First Congressional Church in Torrington and drove around to the back of the building. "What are we doing here?" he asked confused.

"Turn around and look in the back," Dottie instructed. Jay's eyes scanned over the contents in the hatch of the car and saw boxes of baked goods wrapped in plastic bags. He turned back and made eye contact with Dottie in the rearview mirror. "We take all the day-old stuff to the food pantry, and they distribute it to seniors' citizens in the community, and then anyone who comes by on Wednesdays for their weekly groceries. It's the bakery's way of giving back to the community. I usually end up baking a little something special as well to send along to the senior center for their luncheon. The Perino's have been doing this for as long as I can remember. Delivering the day olds was one of Scottie's first jobs when he got his driver's license. I'm surprised he never mentioned it."

"Maybe he did," Jay said. "I don't really remember." Jay helped take boxes into the basement kitchen where a team of volunteers were preparing lunch to be driven over to the senior center. He spent the afternoon helping to pack lunches, deliver and serve them to the seniors and clean up afterwards. By the time they were done it was almost two o'clock. Three hours had flown by. The elderly were laughing and sharing stories with him about their good old days. Once back in Dottie's car, he had a moment to reflect on the afternoon. He had a smile on his face, accomplishment and joy filled his heart. He made eye contact with Dottie in the rear-view mirror. They smiled at each other while Viv chattered on and on about all the gossip she overheard while at the senior center.

They pulled up into River's Edge parking lot to bring Viv

back for her afternoon naptime. "Do you mind if I go in and say hi to Em?" Jay asked.

"We expect you to," Viv said opening her car door before the car had come to a full stop.

"Jesus, Viv, will you at least wait until I put the car in park," Dottie said aggravated with her sister. Viv walked as fast as her shuffling feet and cane could carry her to the front door.

"It's naptime, Dottie. I need my beauty sleep so I can be refreshed for dinner and game night."

Dottie walked around to the front of the car joining Jay. "I love my sister. I really do, but sometimes there's only so much Viv one can take in a day." Jay and Dottie walked through the double doors, signed in at the front desk and proceeded down the hall. Emmaline was standing at the nurses' station writing on a whiteboard on the wall when they approached. She turned toward them, her expression changed from deep thought to surprised.

"Hey, what are you doing here?" She directed her question to Jay as she walked out from behind the desk, wrapping one arm around Jay giving him a half hug.

"Your mom and aunt showed up to the cabin, forced me to drink tea, and then dragged me to the senior center to serve lunches and wash dishes."

"And he loved every minute of it." Dottie smiled at the both of them before turning to walk down the hall to make sure Viv made it into her own room and not someone else's. Something that had happened before. Many a resident had found Viv crashed out in their beds when she got confused. Jay and Em watched Dottie walk away.

"She's right. I enjoyed it. I was so busy I didn't have time to think about the fact I'm not working or to feel sorry for myself and my rattled brain. I felt like...like I had purpose." Jay gave her side a squeeze.

"I'm so happy for you. Maybe you could do more of it. Mom is retired but you would never know it. Between her bread orders from Perino's and her volunteer work, she is busier now than she was when she was working full time." Dottie walked back down the hall to them. She gave Em a hug and grabbed Jay's shirt sleeve.

"Time to go. I have some prep to do for tomorrow's batch. Emmy, I'm snagging your husband a few more days this week. I've got a busy week ahead and could use his help." Dottie looked up at Jay. "Walking club meets at the bike trail at eight a.m. tomorrow after bread drop off. Then we have to go make a new batch of dough to let rise. I'll teach you how to make sourdough first and we can go on from there. But enough for today, don't want to overwhelm you on your first day." Dottie kept talking about their agenda for the week as she drove him home.

Jay wasn't sure what had happened, but it made him happy he had something to do. He knew Emmaline was getting frustrated finding him in the same spot when she got home as when she had left. She never said it, but he could tell by her disappointed sigh when she said hello. He was getting sick of himself too. He wanted to get out of his funk. Maybe helping Dottie was just what he needed to focus on getting better and show everyone he was ready to get back to work after the holidays.

CHAPTER NINETEEN
Emmaline

Josie walked up behind Emmaline who was watching her mother and husband walk out the door of her work. "What was that all about?" she asked.

"Mom took Jay out for the day to help with the senior lunches and day-old deliveries."

"No way. Good for her." Josie pulled her phone out of her scrub pocket. "Time for my lunch break."

"Enjoy," Em said walking back around the desk returning to her whiteboard. Josie followed her. She stood next to Emmaline and leaned in towards her.

"Have you told him?" Emmaline turned toward her friend and shook her head side-to-side. "Em, you have to tell him at some point. You're going to start to show."

"I know. There just never seems to be a good time and then I was thinking..." She leaned her mouth closer to Josie's ear. "Christmas is only a couple of weeks away. I was thinking of telling him on Christmas morning." Josie let out a squeal, then covered her mouth to catch herself. Em laughed with a mischievous grin on her face. "I was thinking of wrapping a baby sized

Red Sox uniform with a little baseball glove holding the pregnancy stick. What do you think?"

"Oh my god," Josie said like Janice from Friends. "Em, I love it! I fucking love it! He's going to totally lose his shit when he sees it. Best gift ever. Full circle. You got married at the Red Sox and announce your pregnancy to him with the Sox. It's perfect. *Eek*...I can't wait. Try to record it so I can see his reaction." Josie was hopping up and down on the balls of her feet. Emmaline couldn't keep the smile off of her own face or she felt the excitement down to her belly or was it another bout of nausea coming. She couldn't tell.

"I'll do my best. I'm excited. Hopefully hanging out with my mom will help him get out of this recent funk and Christmas will be the turning point for better days." Emmaline not only spoke the words but wished for them in her heart. She wanted, no needed, things to start getting better. She had been hiding her morning sickness from Jay, but she knew she couldn't hide her pregnancy from him much longer.

"Wait, aren't you working on Christmas?" Josie stopped bouncing, turning to her friend with concern across her brow.

"Yes, but not until eleven. I'm going to tell him in the morning. It will give us something extra special to celebrate when I get home after work."

"I'm so happy for you, Em. I can't wait to be an aunty. Are you taking your folic acid? Have you gone for an ultrasound yet? If you need a birthing partner, you know I'm here."

"Oh, my goodness, Josie, slow down and shh...quiet down. Yes, I'm taking my folic acid. I have had one ultrasound to confirm the pregnancy and hear the heartbeat. I'm sure Jay would want to be my birthing partner, but if I need a sub, you'll be the first person I call."

Josie grabbed her into a hug and squeezed her tight. Then she dropped the paper she was holding in her hand onto the floor. When she bent to pick it up, she whispered to Emmaline's stomach, "I am going to spoil you rotten, little one. I can't wait. Remember, Aunt Josie. I'm your favorite." Emmaline laughed and went back to her whiteboard which should have been finished a while ago.

The next few weeks before Christmas were a blur. Between decorating the nursing home and the cabin, Christmas shopping, gift wrapping, cookie swaps, and the high and lows of Jay's moods Emmaline was exhausted. He did his best on the days he spent with Dottie. When he was left by himself, he slipped back into his inner darkness. When Emmaline mentioned her concerns, he would repeat how he needed to get back to work. He would say he wasn't good by himself. They attended the Christmas party at her work together, but it was too overstimulating for him. The lights, music, dancing, food being handed around to everyone everywhere, Viv and her antics. Jay was trying to stick it out, but Emmaline could see the migraine forming on his pained face. His eyes winced at the lights and sounds. She used herself as an excuse and left before the party ended. She didn't mind leaving as she was starting to have aversions to certain smells and something in the dining room was making her stomach turn. She wanted to get out of there before it caused her to vomit.

They were invited to the Christmas party for Jay's work and another at the brewery with their friends. Emmaline declined them both on their behalf. She didn't need to put them both through the discomfort of not knowing how their bodies would react to the situations. As Christmas grew closer, Emmaline was getting excited for her surprise. She ordered the newborn baseball outfit and glove and had it shipped to Josie's house. Their tradition was to wrap all their gifts at Josie's place while drinking too much wine and watching Hallmark Channel's Countdown to Christmas. They spent the Sunday before Christmas doing just that while Jay was watching football at the cabin with his group of friends. This felt normal to Emmaline. She hadn't been this happy or excited since the drive to Fenway Park to get married.

Since Emmaline was pregnant and couldn't drink Josie made special mocktails for her. Josie got drunk while her cat climbed all over their wrapping paper and played with the ribbons and bows. Emmaline ate lace after lace of Twizzlers. This was her first craving, and she couldn't get enough of its strawberry flavor. She even bit off both ends of one lace and stuck it in her sparkling mocktail as a straw. Josie ended up passing out on the couch before their third movie had ended. Emmaline cleaned the last bits of the Christmas wrapping mess, covered her friend in a blanket and made sure the cat had food and water.

She grabbed a sticky note off the counter and a pen. *Don't forget dinner is at the cabin tomorrow night at 6. Drink water and take some Tylenol when you wake up. Love ya xoxo.*

When she got home she found Jay at the kitchen sink cleaning up from his game day feast. "Hey babe, how was the game?"

"Great, we beat the Jets by twelve. I can't wait to rub it in Bonetti's face when I see him at work." Jay paused realizing what he said. "I mean when I see him next."

"Congrats. Did you and the guys have a good time?"

"A really good time. It was great having everyone over here, hanging out."

Emmaline walked over to Jay squeezing him from behind. "I'm so happy for you." She stood on her tiptoes and kissed his cheek. "I'm going to take a hot shower and climb into bed. Tomorrow is a busy day."

"Anything I can do to help?"

"I can't think of anything right now, but I'm sure there is. Mom and Viv are bringing desserts. I'll put the turkey in the oven early in the morning. The Perino's are bringing garlic mashed potatoes and homemade cranberry sauce."

"Oh," Jay said rolling his eyes in pleasure. "I love Mrs. Perino's cranberry sauce. I could eat the whole bowl by myself."

"Then I think you will be sitting on the other side of the table from it," she teased. "Scottie's bringing extra tables and chairs. I'm not sure who is coming from our friend group. I left it open-ended and told them to stop by if they could. I've got the stuffing, gravy, and veggies covered so I think we are good." Em turned to walk up the stairs.

"What about drinks, alcohol?" Jay asked. Emmaline had completely forgotten about alcohol since she was not drinking. She also hadn't thought about how she would hide her not drinking from Jay and the others. She'd have to figure it out before dinner the next night as Mr. Perino would make a toast before the meal.

"Yikes. I was so busy with the food I forgot about the drinks. Maybe you could take care of it for me tomorrow?" she asked while heading up the stairs.

"You bet." She heard Jay say as she slipped down the hallway and into their bathroom.

Emmaline undressed for her shower and stared at her naked form in the mirror. Turning to the side, she noticed a little bulge had begun to pop out. She made circles on her belly with a loving touch. "Only two more days, little one, then we can celebrate you." Emmaline couldn't wait to tell Jay. She hated keeping secrets from him. They were in such a good place right now. Her hope was it would keep getting better once he knew, and they could start preparing for their first baby together.

◦ ~ ◦

The next morning, Emmaline was in the kitchen prepping the turkey when Jay came down. She watched his movements as he made his way around the island. He made a cup of tea, took one sip, and poured it out. He rinsed his mug and then went to the Keurig, making himself coffee instead. She didn't say anything. She thought he was giving himself a Christmas treat. "Did you make a list for me?" he barked toward her.

She was taken aback by his tone. "No, but I can do it now."

"You know the liquor store is going to be packed today, Em. I need to get there early." He grabbed his coffee, and a cinnamon roll she had made earlier. Without saying a word, he headed back up the stairs. She listened as the shower was turned on. *Please, don't let this be a mistake. Maybe hosting Christmas Eve dinner was a bad idea.* She prayed Jay would get out of his funk while she wrote out a list of the beverages they would need for the evening.

Jay came down after his shower, seeming a little better than he was before it. *A shower and coffee work for me too.* Emmaline grabbed the list she had made from the counter and walked it over to him. "All set. Can you take a look and see if I missed anything?"

"I'm sure it's fine. But if I see anything else, I'll grab it while I'm at the store. Call me if you think of anything else you need."

"Will do. Drive safely. Love you." She stood on her tiptoes to kiss him.

"Love you too," he reciprocated and bent down to meet her lips, barely grazing them. He grabbed his winter coat and tan Carhartt beanie cap from the hook and headed out the door. "Emmaline watched Jake trot over to the window, watching Jay leave as if to ask, 'What about me?'

Emmaline glanced down at their boy, "Come on Jake. Let's go for a walk." As soon as the dog heard the word walk, he recovered from his disappointment and raced to the back door.

CHAPTER TWENTY

Jay

Even months after the accident, Jay still got anxious getting behind the wheel of a vehicle. He was always a cautious driver before. As a police officer he felt an obligation to lead by example, especially out on public roads. He drove the windy roads into the main part of town to Valley Spirit Shop, the local liquor store in town. He had been extremely agitated since he woke up, like he was on edge about something happening. There were going to be a lot of people in the cabin that night for dinner, but they were all like family to him. Was it the pressure of entertaining, of Christmas or the anxiety in the air? He couldn't put his finger on it, but his anxiety was taking over his nervous system.

Jay took a deep breath and tried to focus on the road ahead of him. There was a lot of traffic out because of the holiday, even in their small town, the roads seemed extra congested. Jay pulled into the parking lot of the liquor store. It was in the same strip mall as a grocery store. Between last minute grocery shopping and liquor store runs, Jay had a hard time finding a parking spot. He drove around the lot a few times and had to stop for women with shopping carts full of food, Dads holding hands of small children crossing in front of him, and other cars also searching for a place to park. His heart raced in his chest. There were too many people, too much movement. He was struggling to keep track of where he should go next until a car beeped at him from behind. He hadn't realized he had come to a complete stop. He started inching his truck forward down the row of full spots. He needed to get out of all of the congestion. He decided to park in the back of the strip mall.

Once parked, he kept his head down as he walked around the back of the building to the liquor store's front door. He heard the ding of the door as he entered, but he kept his gaze down. Even though he heard someone say, "Merry Christmas." Instead of returning the greeting, he pulled the list from Emmaline out of his front pocket, picked up a shopping basket, and focused on filling it with items on the list.

After paying for his purchases, he felt such relief to be leaving the complex. He wanted to get back home to the comfort of Emmaline, Jake, and their cabin. As Jay drove down route 44 in New Hartford, he noticed the cars in front of him slowing down and police activity further up ahead. He slowed his truck down as he got closer and realized there was an accident up ahead, traffic was being rerouted. Jay looked up at the flashing lights of police vehicles, he saw an ambulance and fire truck as well. He slowed to a stop. He was having trouble catching his breath, his heart was beating fast, and his eyes were blurring. He put his head down on the top of the steering wheel trying to compose himself. A loud honk from behind his truck caused him to jump in shock. As he lifted his head and gazed out the windshield a flash of Cecelia's face came into his mind, the last image of her alive.

On autopilot, Jay followed the car in front of him to wherever it was being redirected. Once out of the traffic on the main road and moving on the back streets, Jay pulled over to the side of the road in front of an old New England Victorian house. He turned the truck off and sat there trying to regulate his heartbeat and breath. He looked around at the houses on the street. He had never experienced anything like this. He didn't know where he was. He didn't recognize the houses on the street or the street itself. He pulled his cell phone out of his front pocket and called Emmaline. She answered on the second ring.

"Hey babe, did you get everything?"

"Em, something's wrong with me," he moved his head making eye contact with each house on the street around him. "I don't know where I am."

"It's okay. I got you. I'll help you," Jay heard her tone switch from happy when she answered to one of concern. "Look at your surroundings and tell me what you see. Any street signs?"

Jay glanced around at his surroundings. He saw a street sign up ahead of him, but he couldn't read it. "Yeah, it's too far away though."

"Do you feel comfortable driving to it or even getting out of the truck and walking over to it?"

"I...I can drive to it," he stammered breathlessly while his heart beat fast in his chest. He slowly put the truck in drive and approached the end of the street where the signs at the cross-section were hanging. "One says Wickett Street and the other says Black Bridge Road."

"I know where you are. Go onto Black Bridge and I will guide you home from there." Jay took comfort in the strength he heard in Emmaline's voice. Without saying it, she was reassuring him he was going to be okay. He would be home soon. He followed her directions as she guided him with her soft, comforting voice back to their driveway. When he pulled in, she was standing in the driveway in the cold December air waiting for him. He barely put his truck in park when he jumped out and ran into her arms. She held him as if he were a lost child finally found.

Emmaline slowly guided him into the cabin to a chair before returning to the truck to unload the alcohol. Jay watched her as she walked back out. He was trying to get his mind straight by closing his eyes and gently shaking his head side-to-side. Over the course of the past thirty minutes a migraine had formed pulsating across his forehead and temples. He got up and went to the cabinet to get a couple of Advil. "Why don't you go lie down for a bit. Nobody will be here for a while." He heard Emmaline slowly approach from behind.

"Good idea. I think I will." Without even turning around he moved from the counter, up the stairs, and straight into their bedroom. He kicked his shoes off listening to them drop to the floor. He felt movement as Jake jumped on the bed circling around until he found a comfy spot of his own. With all of the stress the morning brought on to his central nervous system and body, Jay fell asleep fast.

Jay woke up to the sounds of voices and laughter. It took him a moment to remember where he was and what day it was. He blinked his eyes open, glancing outside the window next to his bedside table. It was dark outside. He had slept the whole afternoon away. Slowly sitting up, he could make out the sounds from the familiar voices. He knew he needed to collect his composure from the morning before heading down to greet everyone. The last thing he felt like doing was entertaining a houseful of people, even if they were all the people he loved. He slowly rose to his feet and headed into the bathroom. As he stood in front of the sink, he glanced at his reflection in the mirror. A stranger with sad eyes and a pale face stared back at him. Jay splashed some water on himself. His insides were still twisted up from what happened earlier in the day. How was it possible for him to forget the town he lived in and how to get back to the house he built with his own hands? Part of him was sad about what occurred, and the other part was angry his brain could not access the information that had been stored in there for over two decades. To make it through the evening, Jay would need to push all those feelings aside, put on a smile, and pretend to be the happy-go-lucky guy they all loved.

CHAPTER TWENTY-ONE

Emmaline

Emmaline turned her head from the pot of gravy she was stirring. She heard footsteps coming down the stairs. As Jay walked down, the group of family and friends yelled his name with a round of "Merry Christmas" to him. Emmaline watched his facial expression. She knew that smile, it was his fake smile he put on when he didn't want to be somewhere or was waiting for something to end. His polite smile, the tone of his "Merry Christmas" he said in return told her he still hadn't gotten over what happened earlier. It had scared her. She couldn't imagine how it was affecting him.

She walked over to the foot of the stairs. "Hey babe, is your headache any better?" She prompted him so he would know what she had told everyone when they arrived, and he wasn't there.

"Much better, thanks," He leaned down and kissed her on her cheek. "I'm ready for a beer and some turkey." He laughed out loud. Emmaline saw the laughter didn't reach his eyes.

"Scottie can help you with the first, unfortunately, you'll have to wait another hour for turkey. There are appetizers out though.

Mingle with everyone while I finish up." She gave him a quick squeeze, turned, and walked back to the stove. Josie walked over and stood by her side like she was admiring Emmaline's skill at stirring gravy.

"Are you excited for tomorrow morning?" Emmaline didn't look over at her friend. Her stomach dropped; her heart sank. She was doubting if tomorrow was a suitable time to tell Jay now. She shook her head yes and smiled, keeping her gaze down at the pot in front of her. She knew if she made eye contact with her best friend, Josie would know immediately something was wrong.

"Josie," Mrs. Perino shouted from across the kitchen island. "When are you and my son going to finally get together. He's a good boy; he has a good job; he would be a great match for you."

Emmaline and Josie turned around at the same time. Smiles spreading across both of their faces. Emmaline glanced over at Scottie who was laughing. "I agree with you, Mrs. Perino," Josie said to the older woman. "But unfortunately for Scottie, he's not my type. I like women."

"Oh, well in that case. I've got a great woman for you. My niece. She's a lesbian too. She's beautiful, has a great job and would be a great match for you. Come over here and I'll show her to you on the Facebook." Everyone was laughing at this point at how easily Mrs. Perino could switch gears with her matchmaking. Josie turned to Emmaline, shrugging in resignation, and walked over to where Mrs. Perino was sitting so she could see her niece on 'The Facebook.'

Emmaline looked around the room with a grateful smile on her face. Her mom and aunt were chatting it up with Mr. Perino. Scottie and Jay stood by the fireplace laughing with beers in their hands, probably reminiscing over earlier times in their childhood. Josie's younger brother, Matteo, was playing with

Jake. Her world appeared perfect from the outside in. She wished she could shake the sickening feeling building up in her gut.

The hour passed by quickly, the turkey and all of the fixings were ready. It was time to carve the turkey. Emmaline signaled Jay by pointing to the electric carving knife on the counter. Jay took his cue and headed over to it. She laid out the platter for the carvings and plugged in the appliance. As Jay turned it on, a load sound like a drill at a dentist's office shrieked at them. Jay dropped the carver onto the counter and held his ears. Emmaline quickly reached over and turned it off. She glanced up at Jay trying to take him in her arms to comfort him, but he pushed her away.

"No...don't," he said with a bit of anger in his voice. "I'm fine. I wasn't expecting it to be so loud." Jay turned around; Emmaline saw all eyes staring at the two of them. "Mr. Perino, why don't you carve the turkey this year. I always make such a mess out of it. I'm sure being a baker you are much better with a carving knife than I am." Emmaline was impressed by how quickly everyone recovered or pretended to.

"I'd be honored. Thank you, son." Mr. Perino carved perfect slices of turkey, placing them exquisitely aligned on the platter.

Dinner went fine and the food was delicious, but there was a shift in the air. She wasn't sure if it was really there, or she was projecting her own inner feelings outward. There was a lot of laughter, storytelling, and way too much food eaten. Some of their other friends stop by for dessert. By ten o'clock, they all said their goodbyes with content expressions on their faces, satiated with food and conversation. While standing at the door waving with their black lab by their side, Emmaline and Jay thanked everyone for coming, wishing them all a Merry Christmas one last time. A picture-perfect moment.

After closing the door, they both quietly went to clean up the dining area and kitchen. Her mom and aunt had done most of the dishes. There were a few things left over from dessert. "You cooked all day. I've got this," he took the stack of dessert plates she had collected off the table from her.

"Are you sure?"

"Yes, go rest. Put your feet up. I've got it." She started to walk over to the couch when she heard a loud crash and Jay yell out, "God dammit!" Emmaline turned back and saw the handful of plates she had given to Jay broken all over the floor.

"What the fuck is wrong with me?" Emmaline bent down to start cleaning up the mess. "No, I got this. It's my mess. Jake, back away." She heard the anger in his voice as he shoved Jake away from the broken shards of ceramic.

"It's okay, babe. Accidents happen."

"It's not okay. Stop talking to me like everything is okay. It's not. My brain is all fucked up and I hate it. I absolutely hate it." Jay was screaming now; at a volume Emmaline had never heard from him. At this point, he had the dustpan and small broom out and was cleaning up the mess. Emmaline was squatting down in front of him.

Quietly, she spoke to him, "Maybe it's time to make an appointment with Dr. Jim's office."

Jay stood up abruptly, dumping the contents of the dustpan in the trash. "Jesus, Em. Really. You're going to bring that up now." He dropped the dustpan and stormed up the stairs. "Merry fucking Christmas!" he yelled down at her.

"Jay, wait. I didn't mean anything by it. I can see how frustrated you've been today. I thought Dr. Jim would be someone who could understand better than I can." Her words traveled with her up the stairs as she followed him. When she reached the top of the stairs, she placed her hand on his back. Jay quickly turned to swat her hand away. Emmaline lost her balance and began slipping backward down the stairs. She tried to grab onto the railing to help stop her fall. Her eyes met Jay's; he stared back at her with a look of shock. As she continued to fall backward finally coming to a stop on the hardwood floor landing harshly on her tailbone, all she could think about was her baby.

Jay

Jay raced down the stairs after Emmaline trying to catch her while she slid backward. He held onto the handrail with one hand and tried to catch his wife with the other. She stared up at him with fear, shock, and then sadness in her eyes. Jay's heart was beating fast.

"Oh my god, Em. I'm so sorry. Are you okay?"

Emmaline stood up slowly righting herself. She looked at him like he was someone she didn't know. Jay wasn't sure if he knew who he was.

"I'm fine," she said, not reaching for his hand. She straightened the cranberry red dress she was wearing. Closing her eyes, she took a breath, then stared up at Jay. "I'm going to my mom's house tonight. Give you some time. It's obvious you're not feeling well and maybe a nice quiet house is what you need. Then I won't wake you in the morning when I get ready for work."

He stood there speechless as Emmaline walked by him up the stairs. He heard her rustling around in her dresser and then the zip of a bag being closed. She walked back down the stairs without a word, grabbing her purse and her keys before heading out the door and slowly closing it behind her.

With his head bowed, Jay walked to the top of the stairs. He didn't care about cleaning the remains of the night up, he didn't care about turning the lights off downstairs or letting Jake out one more time. He wanted to crawl into bed, close his eyes, and imagine this day never happened. Jay didn't like who he was becoming. He felt like Bruce Banner turning into the Hulk. One moment he was fine and then this creature took over his body and mind. He didn't know how to control it or how to stop it. He couldn't believe he put his hands on Emmaline. He couldn't believe he shoved her so hard she fell down the stairs. He stood against the hallway wall and slowly sank down with the bottom of his fist hitting the floor in frustration. *What is wrong with me? I don't know who I am anymore.* He internally screamed at himself as he clasped his fingers into his hair and squeezed his head.

He slowly pulled his hands down. He sat on the floor in their upstairs hallway, back propped up against the wall, legs bent, feet planted, and he stared at his hands stretched out in front of him.

I want to be stronger than my father. He went down a black hole after his accident. How do I stop myself from doing the same? Gentle tears began to fall from his eyes, then ugly tears as sadness overtook him. He didn't know what to do. He felt so helpless. A feeling he hadn't had since he was a child. He and his mother watching his father suffer in pain unable do anything to help him. Here he is the one in pain and he's also the one not doing anything about it. This brain injury was turning him into someone he didn't like, someone he didn't know. He knew he needed to find the determination to fix this, he didn't want to lose his wife. He loved Emmaline. She was his everything.

He still feared taking medication. He did not want to be like his father. He did not want to take the chance of becoming addicted. There must be something he could do to keep himself from turning into a horrible beast. The version of himself that came out tonight. He didn't like it. As Jay continued to weep, he picked himself up off the beautiful hardwood floor he laid with his own hands and walked into his bedroom. He climbed into the queen-size bed he shared with Em and knew it was time. He needed help. A new resolve washed over Jay. A determination he hadn't felt in a long time. An old part of himself wanted to resurface. The resilient part that knew how to overcome.

He grabbed his phone off the bedside table, then opened the drawer, and pulled out the business card which had been sitting there for months. He punched in the cell phone number Dr. Jim wrote on the back of the card. He typed three words into the message bar.

Jay: "I need help."

But he didn't hit send.

CHAPTER TWENTY-TWO

Emmaline

Emmaline walked into the living room of the house she grew up in. She stood at the entrance, glancing around the room at the furniture. Her eyes moved across to the brown, leather chair and matching ottoman. The brown, leather chair still held the indentation from where her father used to sit. The place he used to bark orders to her and her mother. She walked over to the back of it and ran her hand across the top.

"How come you never got rid of this chair," she asked her mother as she walked around to the front of it. Her mother walked over to the chair and sat right down in the spot where her ex-husband who abused her sat. She leaned forward a little and slid open the drawer of the end table. Dottie pulled out a child-sized plastic crown and placed it on her head in a dramatic fashion. She sat back in the chair with a smile on her face, propping her feet on top of the ottoman.

"Because I took my power back. I am the queen of this castle," she stated emphatically. Emmaline had a new appreciation for how far her mother had come. "Do you want to tell me what happened?"

Emmaline filled her mother in on the events of the day from Jay not being able to find his way home to her falling down the stairs. Dottie listened without interrupting and without judgement on her face. "I got scared, Mom. What if?" Emmaline turned her head away from her mother pausing for a few beats. "What if Jay turns out to be like Dad?"

"You and Jay, you are not your father and me. You have a love we never had. You have a partnership we never had. There is a significant difference between love for need and a love that is true. We all change as we age. It's growing and accepting this change. You need to find a way to do it together. Your father and I couldn't. I thought I could help him. I thought I could change him. I didn't understand how sick he was. We were frustrated with each other. His mental illness went undiagnosed for too long. Believe me when I tell you the abuse was not one way. You remember the physical abuse from him when he was having an episode. But I wasn't innocent in the situation. I can admit I verbally abused him. I knew how to push his buttons. There was a lot of 'why can't you do this' and 'why can't you be this way' or 'what is wrong with you.' I was so uneducated in his needs. I didn't want to see what was right in front of my face. He needed help, and not from me. Emmaline, I didn't understand. I didn't take the time to find your dad the help he needed. With you and Jay, it can work out, it will work out. Lean on each other and not away from one another. I know it down to my core. You both will figure this all out."

Emmaline reached down and grabbed her mother's hand and gave it a squeeze as tears flooded her eyes. Her heart wanted to believe her mother's words so badly, but scars left behind from old memories still hurt. She was tired. She wanted to crawl into her childhood bed, go to sleep, and wake up to a new day. Maybe a new perspective on the future that is different than the one they planned together not so long ago.

Emmaline woke up the next morning and cried in bed. She couldn't muster up the energy to go for her usual morning run. She decided to go into work early instead. It was a good choice, considering how needy all the patients were when she got in. It felt more like there was a full moon happening instead of Christmas. One patient wanted her to call a van to take him to the movies, another wanted more blankets because her room was too cold, another wanted an additional shower because she had spilt her soup on herself and felt sticky. Even though she felt she was running in circles from room to room, it was a good distraction to keep her mind off the night before.

Aunt Viv was having a day as well, but a vastly different kind of day. She had packed all her belongings into a suitcase, got dressed up in her fanciest dress, sunglasses, and sun hat. She thought she was going on vacation to Hawaii. The staff didn't want to disappoint her, so they brought her out to the sunroom and set up a chair for her to lounge in. They also brought her a fruity seltzer with a straw and a cherry in it which made her extremely happy. A few of the other patients decided to join her. Even Viv's boyfriend, Roger, put on a Hawaiian shirt he happened to have in his closet. It was a Hawaiian Christmas at River's Edge.

Needless to say, they were keeping Emmaline occupied and entertained for the morning. When she finally got to take her lunch break, she pulled out her cell phone and noticed the unread text from Jay. She read it a couple times with tears forming in her eyes. She wasn't sure if she should text back or not so she sat and ate her lunch ruminating in her head on how she should reply. She finally thought of what she wanted to say. She carefully typed the words on her phone, deleted them and retyped them a few more times. She wanted to make sure she was clear about what she was trying to say. She wanted to be supportive of him and what he's going through, and yet she needed to be cautious for herself and her baby. The baby she never got to tell him about that morning. She hit send as the door to the break room opened. Josie poked her head in. "Sorry to interrupt your break, but we need your help. Viv decided she wanted to go skinny-dipping in the ocean. She took all her clothes off and now she's sitting in the middle of the outdoor water fountain with three other patients. It's forty-two degrees out, and they don't even care. Guess they wanted a cold plunge."

Emmaline started laughing as Josie continued, "We're going to need your help getting them dried off and back in their clothes." Emmaline tucked her phone back into the pocket of her scrubs, stood up and followed her friend out of the lunchroom, laughing to herself at how opposite life can be at times.

Emmaline felt her phone buzz when a message came in. Her heart pounded in anticipation of what his response might be. She couldn't read it until she helped Josie and the two other LPNs on duty get the patients settled into warm clothes. After everyone was situated, Em pulled her phone out of her scrubs pocket and read the message.

Jay: I'm outside in the parking lot. Can we talk for a minute?

She started to type back, then decided it would be better to just go talk to him. She emerged through the automatic front doors. She made eye contact with him through the windshield of his truck. Her heart was beating with a mix of love and nerves. Jay got out of his truck and walked over to her.

"Hi," he said tentatively.

"Hi," she said wrapping her open cardigan around herself as she slowly approached him.

"Em, I am so, so sorry about last night. I don't know what came over me."

"I know."

"I'm going to work on it. I'm going to work on controlling my crazy outbursts. I'm going to work on the anxiety and irritability. I need you by my side. I need you home with me. After you left last night, I got out the card from Dr. Jim. I can't fix this on my own. I see that now. I need help. I'm going to get help. I promise—"

Emmaline raised her hand. "Jay, I'm pregnant." She dropped her head down toward the ground and then slowly lifted it back up.

Jay was speechless. She watched as excitement washed over his face and then slowly changed to concern. He stepped toward her, arms outstretched to give her a hug. She flinched and stepped away from him. Her reaction to him was one she could tell he was not expecting. She saw the hurt in his eyes.

"Please, don't. I can't. I love you so much, Jay. I do. But growing up with an abusive father is something I never wanted my own children to experience. You really scared me last night. I can't take a chance with our baby. I need you to get help, Jay. I have to think of the safety of our baby now. Between my morning sickness and your injury, I can't take care of all three of us." Tears were streaming down Emmaline's face. She knew it broke his heart to see her cry and not be able to comfort her. She knew his instinct was to be a protector.

"It is so hard for me to not be able to make things better for you. It hurts me to see you in pain. It's slowly killing me to see you suffering and not be able to do anything about it. I love you so much. But now, now I have our baby to think about. Please, I'm begging you Jay, take this time and get better. Jim and his team can help you. This is so hard for me to say, but I won't come home until you get real help. This has gone on too long, and it's only gotten worse. I'm going to stay with my mom for a while." Emmaline used the sleeve of her cardigan to wipe the tears off her face. She started to turn back to the entrance.

"Em, wait..." She saw the expression on his face, pure heartbreak. "I...I'm going to get help. I'll take care of it after the New Year. I'm going to meet with Dr. Jim and his team. They'll come up with a treatment plan. I'm going to do it. I'm going to get help." He was pleading with her while inching closer. "I've lost my identity as a police officer. I can't lose you. What am I going to do without you?" Jay's eyes brimmed red with tears. Complete defeat washed over his face. Her heart was breaking. She wanted to run to him, comfort him, tell him they'd figure it out together. But she couldn't. She had another life inside of her she needed to focus on now. As if on cue, Emmaline felt the first flutter of her baby inside of her. Tears glossed over her eyes. She gazed up at the sky to keep them from falling.

"Get better, Jay. You're going to get yourself better. For you, for your job, for me, and for our baby." Without waiting for a response, Emmaline turned and walked back into the building.

After her shift ended, she headed back to her mom's house. She couldn't go back to the cabin. She needed time away from Jay. Time to think.

"Hey, you're back," Dottie said when Emmaline walked through the front door into the living room.

"Is that okay? Do you mind if I stay for a little while?"

"Mind? Of course not. This is your home. You can stay whenever or forever or as long as you like. Have you spoken to Jay?" Emmaline saw the concern on her mother's face. She shook her head no. They sat across from each other in silence, staring at the lighted Christmas Tree glowing from the corner of the room.

"Mom, I'm pregnant." Emmaline's tears filled her eyes blurring the glow of the twinkling lights.

"I know."

Emmaline jerked her head toward her mother in surprise. "You know?"

"Viv." Emmaline shook her head yes as if verbally saying it made sense. Viv would have told her. "I was waiting for you to be ready to tell me."

"I don't know what to do, Mom. I want to be there for Jay and help him with his recovery. I'm trying to be patient, but I have another life to think about. Our baby's life. And I've been so sick. Everything makes me nauseous. I picked up take out Chinese food for dinner last week. I got my usual chicken and broccoli; I was so nauseous from the smell of it I had to pull over to the side of the road and vomit. I spilled the rest of the dinner into the woods on the side of the road and hid the container in the outside garbage can when I got home. When Jay asked me where my dinner was, I told him I wasn't hungry. That I had a late lunch. He came to see me at work today and I finally told him I was pregnant."

"You hadn't told him yet?" Dottie looked at her in shock.

"It never was the right time. His moods have been all over the place. I never know which Jay I'm going to get. I planned on telling him today. It was going to be his Christmas present. My pregnancy test wrapped up in a newborn Red Sox outfit." Dottie looked at her in surprise. "But instead, last night happened. When he came by River's Edge today it sort of came out."

Emmaline stood up and began pacing the room. "You should have seen his face, Mom. It was a flash of excitement to extreme sadness. I don't know what to do. I must think of my baby now. I love him so much, but I will not take a chance of Jay having any outbursts and risking harm to our baby like he did last night."

"I understand. I wish I were as brave as you are and had left your father long before I did or had been aware enough to recognize the mental anguish he was living with. We can't live with regrets weighing us down, but there is so much I regret. It's okay for you to take your time to process all of this. It really is. But you have to communicate with Jay. Regardless, if you decide to go home tonight, tomorrow, or next week you must keep communicating with him. This is the first major challenge you both have had to face together. It does not have to destroy what you have. This, my dear, is marriage. From this day forward, for better or worse, how will you get through it...together."

"I know. You're right." Emmaline walked over to the chair she had been sitting in and grabbed her purse off the floor next to it. She pulled her cell phone out of the side pocket and texted Jay.

> **Emmaline:** I'm staying at my mom's. I'll be by to pick up some clothes. I'd appreciate it if you were not home.
>
> **Jay:** Okay.
>
> **Emmaline:** I need some time. I hope you understand.
>
> **Jay:** I do.
>
> **Jay:** I love you.
>
> **Emmaline:** I love you.

Emmaline wanted to cry typing those last three words. Her heart was being ripped out of her chest. At that moment, she felt the flutter of the baby again. She reached down to the spot on her belly. The sadness flipped to tender joy. Whether it was the right time or not, she was in love with this little one growing inside of her.

CHAPTER TWENTY-THREE

Jay

Jay left the nursing home in a daze. Emmaline was pregnant. *Pregnant.* He kept saying it over and over in his head as he drove through the streets of New Hartford. How had he not noticed the signs? Her nausea, the vomiting. He had accused her of being drunk. *I'm such a jerk.* He had completely ignored how tired she was after work when she brought home Subway again. He could have had dinner made for her. He could have been helping her along. They could have been celebrating together. Instead, he had spent the last four months pitying himself. He realized he hadn't even asked her the due date, how far along she was, how she was feeling. Again, he had only been thinking of himself when she told him she was pregnant.

Merry fucking Christmas, Jay. You blew it. Jay arrived home on a beautiful December afternoon to an empty cabin. Jake was there, but it was as if he knew Jay had screwed up. He didn't bother to get up from his dog bed when Jay walked in. He just lifted his head to acknowledge Jay's presence and then placed it back down. Jay took off his shoes, hung up his coat, and glanced around their open floor living space. It was decorated for holiday festivities, but the air was filled with loneliness and despair. Jay dragged himself over to the couch. He threw himself down onto it covering his face with his crossed arms. He wasn't sure how long he stayed there. Whether he fell asleep or not. His mind kept wandering back to the moment when Emmaline told him she was pregnant. The scene kept playing over and over in his head. Around seven o'clock, there was a knock on the door. Jay jumped up off the couch in hopes it would be Emmaline. He almost stepped on Jake in his rush to the door. He opened it in anticipation and found Scottie standing on the other side.

"Merry Christmas...ho, ho, ho." His best friend bellowed as he wheeled a road bike through the front door with a big, red bow on the handlebars and a Santa hat on his head.

"Hey," Jay said gloomily.

"Whoa, what happened to you? Was Santa not good to you this year? Did he leave coal in your stocking?" Scottie leaned the bike against the kitchen table and followed Jay as they both walked over to the couch.

"Emmaline's pregnant," Jay replied somberly while running his fingers through his hair, forearms resting on his knees.

"Oh my god, bro, that's fantastic. Congratulations," Scottie gave him a congratulatory pat on the back. "I would think you'd be happier."

"I want to be happier." Jay filled Scottie in on the events from the past two days. Starting with him waking up and not feeling right to when he pushed Emmaline away and she fell down the stairs. "Then she grabbed an overnight bag and went to her mom's. I drove over to River's Edge this morning to apologize and that's when she told me."

"Jesus, man," Scottie said removing the Santa hat from his head. "You can't catch a break. I'm sure you guys can talk it over when she gets home from work. Then the celebrating can begin."

"She's not coming home. She told me she's going to stay at

her mom's for a while. You should have seen her face when she hit the floor and then stared back up at me. There was a moment she looked at me like she was afraid of me. It was a look of pure fear. You know the history with her dad. I don't know what came over me. I was so angry with myself. With this stupid brain of mine when she tried to console me, I shoved her. Scottie, I am not an abuser. I'm not that guy…or am I? Is this the person I'm becoming? Bruce Banner to the Incredible Hulk when I get angry."

Jay turned his head toward his best friend and could see Scottie searching for words of comfort but not finding anything to say. "Jay, I've known you almost your whole life. I can reassure you; you are not an abuser. You have a lot going on. I know you don't want to hear it again, but you need to get help. What's happening to you is not going to go away, but you can learn to manage it and live with it."

Jay stared off into the distance absorbing his friends' words. "Thanks, man. I appreciate it. I really do. I think I need to be alone right now to sort some things out. I hope you understand. I have no Christmas cheer in me today."

"It's okay, Jay. I totally get it." Scottie rose from the couch straightening his pant legs. "You know I'm here for you if you need me."

Jay gave his friend a nod and watched him leave. He felt absolutely worthless. When he got the text from Emmaline saying she wasn't coming home and wanted to stop by to get some clothes when he wasn't there, he was not surprised. Fear seeped through him wondering if he had lost his wife and his unborn child.

Jay spent the better part of the week between Christmas and New Year's walking a triangle. He moved from the couch to the kitchen to the bathroom and back. He didn't have the will to climb the stairs to his own bedroom. He stayed in a cocoon of depression on the couch watching mindless TV over and over.

Scottie texted him after he left on Christmas day. He had forgotten to tell Jay about the bike he had brought to him. The bike was a gift from all of Jay's co-workers. Between the station and the firehouse, all his colleagues chipped in money to get him the bike since he wasn't running. They wanted to do something to help him with his recovery. He also told Jay the other part of the gift was on his front porch. He forgot to bring it in with him. The bike with the red bow on it was exactly where Scottie had left it leaning against the kitchen chair. Whatever he left on the front porch remained unknown.

It had been six days without any communication between him and Emmaline. He had reached for his phone many times to call or text her, but he couldn't get himself to hit the send button for either. He wanted to give Emmaline the space she needed. By New Year's Eve, Jay couldn't take it anymore. He finally texted her.

Jay: Happy New Year.

Three dots appeared and then disappeared a few times. He waited unease filling his chest.

Emmaline: Same to you.

He finally asked the question which had been weighing on him for days.

Jay: Will you be coming home soon?

Emmaline: I want to but I'm afraid to.

Jay read her message a few times before responding.

Jay: I understand. I love you. I'm excited about the baby. I wish we could be together to celebrate our little one. I'm making a promise to you. I will get the treatment I need to get better. I don't want you to be afraid of me. My New Year's promise to you is that. What happened on Christmas Eve will NEVER happen again.

Emmaline: I want to believe you. I really do. I'm scared and now I have our baby to think about.

Jay: I get it. I know how important it is that our kids don't ever experience what you did growing up. I'm going to make it happen, Em. I'm going to fix this. I don't want to lose you. I made a promise to you on our wedding day, and I will keep it.

As he typed the message, tears pooled in his eyes and slid down his face. Jake pulled himself off his dog bed and came over to his master to comfort him. Jay patted his best friend's head while he waited for a response from Emmaline.

Emmaline: Prove it to me. I will take care of our baby. You take care of you.

Jay got his orders and knew it was time to listen or lose everything. He stood up and glanced around at their cabin. The house she made a home after she moved in. It was a mess. He was a mess. It was time to get his shit together and he knew it. Before he did anything else, he walked up the stairs to their bedroom, grabbed the business card out of his bedside table and texted Dr. Jim Gottlieb three simple words.

Jay: "I need help."

Three simple words came back.

Dr. Jim: "I can help."

<hr>

After a shower and a quick once over of the house, Jay decided to take Jake out for a walk on the trails behind the cabin. It had been a long time since he made his way out back. The air was crisp on the first day of the new year. Jay could see his breath with each exhale, his nose turned red in the cold. The crip air in his lungs felt refreshing like that first breath of air when your head comes up from out of the water. With his hat on his head and gloves on his hands, he took his time enjoying the sun on his face while Jake made his mark on various trees and plants sniffing as they walked along. Jay was extra careful with his steps on the uneven terrain. Even walking slowly felt good, because he was outdoors, a place he always found comfort in.

When Jay got home, he noticed the shadow of a person through the kitchen window. His heart leaped in his chest. *Emmaline came home.* Even though he was tired from the walk, he picked up his pace toward the back door. He walked through the door in anticipation of scooping Emmaline into the biggest hug. Instead, he found his mother sitting on the couch, as if she had been waiting for him. "Mom, what are you doing here?"

"And a Happy New Year to you too. What do you think I'm doing here? I came to see my son." She patted the cushion next to her as if beckoning him to sit down like she did when he was a kid and needed a good talking to. Jay dutifully made his way to the couch seat next to her. Jake followed behind excitedly to get his pets from Andrea.

"Why didn't you tell me you were coming?"

"I wanted it to be a surprise for both you and Emmaline. My plan was to stay with Dottie, visit some old friends, and celebrate the exciting news. My first grandbaby." He stared at her dumbfounded, not understanding how she already knew about the baby when he had only found out a week ago. "The plan for me was to visit later in January, but then Dottie called me and filled me on the events of Christmas." Jay nodded, understanding her unexpected visit better. Andrea and Dottie formed a unique bond from the first time they met. They had similar backgrounds and troubled marriages. Outside of being in-laws, they had developed a beautiful friendship since the day Jay and Emmaline introduced them over dinner.

"I really messed things up, Mom. She hasn't been back home since Christmas Eve night. Talk about history repeating itself. I'm worried my marriage may be over." Jay's head drooped. Andrea reached over and took her son's hand into her own.

"Honey, I think it's time you and I had a little talk about Dad." He looked at her apprehensively. She started to reflect on the day she and Jay's father met. Jay loved the story of how his parents met and fell in love. She had told him it was love at first sight. There was a magnetic energy pulling them to each other. His father was a tall man with broad shoulders and deep, brown eyes with long lashes, just like Jays. She was a petite, shy girl with little experience with men. Andrea loved to share how Rob's crooked smirk when he was joking around made her heart flutter.

They met in their early twenties. He was a steelworker, and she was a bank teller. The bank she worked at was expanding. Andrea said the first time she saw Rob he was gracefully walking across a beam on the new addition. She was counting out money and saw out of the bank window this figure moving stealthily across the beam. He caught her eye. She said with his low-hanging Carhartt pants and his muscular physique through his white t-shirt, she lost count of the ones in her hand. Jay would pretend to be grossed out when she talked about his dad that way.

She said she watched him work every day and eventually realized he was watching her too. They continued these flirtatious glances until one day, after Andrea's shift ended, she walked out of the bank and saw Rob standing on the sidewalk outside the door. He had his hard hat in his hands and glanced at her with those eyes, the same ones Jay inherited. Shyly he said, "Tomorrow is my last day on this job."

"Oh, really," she said a bit breathless.

"Yeah...and I was wondering, if you'd maybe want to grab dinner sometime?"

She smiled at him. "I would love to. I have nothing to eat at home and was going to grab take out. If you're all done for the day, maybe we could go get a bite now." Andrea wasn't used to being forward, but she knew she wanted this man and wouldn't taking any chances of him disappearing.

They were married one year later. Ten months after, Jay was born. Rob was madly in love with his son and his wife. She said she felt it every day from him. "I loved your father more than anything and to see what he went through after the accident was brutal for me. When the steel beam fell on top of him and crushed his back, it also crushed his will to live. He was in pain all the time. Your dad could not adjust to the limitations of his body. The drugs gave him an easy escape. He became the victim to the opioid epidemic until it finally took his life."

"I want you to remember the father he was before the accident. The one who took you fishing, played games, and wrestled with you. Your love of baseball came from your father. He taught you how to catch and throw, hit a ball out of the field. What happened to your father after his accident does not have to happen to you. Your dad slid down a black hole and did not know how to come back from it. He did not know how to live in his new reality. He didn't fight for himself or us. You need to fight for yourself, for your wife, your baby and for your future. Jay, I don't regret anything about my marriage to your father. We had many wonderful years together and we had you. A part of me will always love him and a part of me wishes he had died the day of the accident because it killed me to see him suffering. I mourned the loss of your father a long time before he was gone. After he passed, a part of me was relieved, because I knew he wasn't suffering anymore. Andrea voice choked up in her throat.

"You have to choose your own path, your own way to heal. To accept where you are now. Regardless of what happened to your dad or what happened to you, as we age, we all change. It's part of living. Choosing how you walk that path and accept the changes is what makes the difference. Your father couldn't let go of who he once was. But you can. Start accepting this version of yourself, love him. Love Jay Robert Ellis. This next chapter may not be the one you and Emmaline had planned on, but who's to say it won't be better. Life works out that way sometimes."

Jay sat with his head bowed letting his mother's words sink in. He knew she was right. He had to accept his limitations. Accept this new version of himself and his head injury. He had to get to know himself again. He hoped Emmaline could love him as he is now.

"Thanks, Mom. I needed to hear this. I'm really glad you're here." He leaned his head on her shoulder.

"Love you, son," She leaned over and kissed the top of his head. "Now what do you say we order take out, watch some holiday movies, then take a long winter's nap."

"Sounds perfect."

Jay spent a quiet day with his mother. They watched *A Christmas Story, Christmas Vacation* and, of course, *Die Hard*. All the holiday classics. They snacked on an exorbitant amount of food they ordered from Pete's Pizza while intermittently napping. Jay's mind kept wondering back to the moment when Emmaline told him she was pregnant. The scene kept playing over and over in his head. Around seven o'clock, there was a knock on the door. Jay grabbed the remote and paused the movie while jumping up to answer the door. His heart skipped a beat in hopes it would be Emmaline. He opened the door while holding his breath and found Scottie standing on the other side.

"Happy New Year!" His best friend bellowed as he walked through the front door with a Frosty the Snowman hat on his head.

"Hello there, Frosty," Jay said with a laugh.

"Well, look who Santa brought you?" Scottie carried in what he had left on the porch the week before. Then he scooped Andrea up in a big bear hug.

"Scottie, my other son. I've missed you," she said returning the hug.

"When did you get here? I didn't even know you were coming."

"No one did except for Dottie. I was going to surprise the kids. It seems like I only surprised one of them. But we can get into that later. I brought gifts from the sunshine state for everyone. Let's open some presents."

"Well, that's exactly why I'm here." Scottie turned back to the road bike. "The crew at the stations chipped in and bought Jay a road bike and trainer to use in the winter months. I figured I'd come over say Happy New Year and help him set it up."

"How nice of all of you. I tell Jay all the time what an amazing extended family you both have in your jobs." Andrea walked over to where her luggage was resting. Jay watched as Scottie set up the bike on the trainer and Andrea unpacked presents from one of the suitcases. All this time everyone around him had been trying to offer their help. Between Dottie and Viv getting him out of the house, Emmaline planning get-togethers with their friends and keeping the routine of their life going to his work colleagues sending him encouraging messages or silly memes to make him laugh and now his mother and Scottie. They all kept showing up for him.

"We're all rooting for you, buddy. Everyone wants you to get better so you can get back to work. They miss you." Jay was touched by the generosity of his colleagues, his other family. He had spent the last four months in a pool of self-pity. Everyone had been trying to help him except for him.

"What is this thing for?" Andrea walked over to the trainer on the floor. She pointed to it with a questioning expression on her face.

"You put the back wheel of the bike on it so you can ride indoors through the winter. No impact with a bike, like with running. It shouldn't hurt his head. Jay, you can get back to exercising. Trying something new." Scottie beamed with pride. Andrea walked over and hugged Scottie once again.

"Jay, you're surrounded by people who really care about you. I know you know and it's also good to be reminded. Now it's time for you to care about you." Jay knew his mother was right. First thing, the next morning he was calling Dr. Jim's office. He would make an appointment to start therapy.

CHAPTER TWENTY-FOUR

Emmaline

"Hello, Emmaline. Wake up." Emmaline was standing at the nurses' station at River's Edge. Aunt Viv was waving her hand in front of Em's face.

"Sorry, Viv. I was off in another world."

"Obviously. Now get your shit together, girly, I've got an agenda for the new year, and I need you to help me."

"O-kay," Emmaline laughed while grabbing a pad of paper off the top of the desk and a pen from her scrub's pocket. "Should I be writing these things down?"

"Yes, great idea. Now come on." She waved for Emmaline to follow her down the hall. "We've got a lot to do. We've got about four and half months before this little one arrives. Georgie!" Viv yelled down the hallway moving as fast as her shuffling feet and cane could carry her. "Georgie, get out here. We need to get started on the quilt for the baby." A hunchbacked woman in her late eighties with salt and pepper hair came shuffling out of the room at the end of the hall. She held pattern books in her hands. "Em, have you thought about a theme for the nursery? It will help with our planning."

Emmaline stopped in her tracks. *Nursery? Four and a half months until the baby arrives.* Emmaline couldn't move. She was frozen still as a wave of anxiety washed over here. Viv turned around when she realized Emmaline was not following her.

"Don't worry, my love. You and your man will have everything worked out by then. Now come on, let's start with colors you like." Vivian walked back to the spot where Em was grounded. She wrapped her arm through Emmaline's and walked her down the hallway. Usually, it would be the other way around. But Emmaline felt helpless and needed her aunt to guide her.

"I'm going to be a mom," she said in shock. "Holy shit, Viv. In less than five months I'm going to be a mom. I'm going to have to take care of another human being." Emmaline peered down at the small pouch which had started to protrude in her belly.

"Yes, you are and you're going to be an amazing mother." Viv patted her hand through their linked arms. "You and that hot hubby of yours are going to get everything worked out, welcome your baby and they all lived happily ever after." Viv sang the last of her words.

Emmaline paused their walking and turned to look at her aunt, tears of sadness pooling in her eyes. "What if it doesn't? What if we can't come back from this? What if I have to raise the baby on my own? What if Jay decides we aren't what he wants anymore? What if..."

Viv reached over and covered Emmaline's mouth with her index finger to shush her. "Stop catastrophizing. It's not going to help you or the baby. One thing at time." Viv turned and walked Emmaline into the sitting room where a group of women were situated in assorted styles of chairs brainstorming ideas for the quilt they would make for her baby.

Emmaline's mind had been reeling all day with what ifs. She was so happy when she finally got back to her mom's house. She needed to call Josie and unpack everything swirling in her brain. She needed Josie to talk her down from her mental ledge.

She said a quick hello to her mother and then headed down the hall to her room. She felt like a teenager with hot gossip she needed to tell her best friend behind her bedroom's closed door. But there were no good stories to share. Emmaline curled up on her childhood bed and hit the send button on her cell phone.

"Hey, mama. How's my favorite pregnant lady doing?" Before Josie could finish the last word, Emmaline started unpacking her interaction with Viv and the other ladies at River's Edge. Then she continued to word vomit all her fears and anxieties. "Whoa, whoa, whoa...slow down. My god you're going to send yourself into early labor. You need to stop thinking of the 'what if's' or you're going to drive yourself crazy. Em, I know how much you like to control things."

"I do not!"

"Yes. You do. Now take a deep breath and listen. You have two important things going on in your life, your marriage, and your baby. Let's not talk about what you can't control. Let's talk about what you can control. You and Jay are working through something right now, correct?"

"Yes, not quite sure what it is exactly our marriage, our future? But yes, we are." If Emmaline still had her old landline phone, she would be twirling her fingers into the cord right then. Instead, she twirled her fingers in her hair with her free hand.

"What you can't control in this situation is the outcome, but what you can control is how you communicate with each other. Em, talk to Jay. A visit, a phone call, a text. Anything to open the lines of communication. I may not know Jay as well as I know you, but I can guess his insides are in as much turmoil as yours are over this. Keep the lines of communication open while you both work on your own stuff. Then maybe, at some point, you can come back together to heal the rest."

"You're right. We've always been able to talk to each other. We need to find our way back to that. What about the baby? In less than five months he or she will be here. What if we haven't figured it out by then? Then what?"

"Again, it's an unknown. Don't stress the unknown. Instead do what you love doing. Start planning for the arrival. You love your lists. Start making lists of what you need for the baby. We could do a baby registry online together. We could go shopping and you could scan all the crazy gadgets you will need like a crib, a car seat, highchair, the weird boogie sucker moms stick in their kid's nose. Regardless of the circumstances, we would have been doing all of it together anyways."

Emmaline laughed at her friend. Josie knew how to get her out of her funk. "You're right. My thoughts won't stop pinging all over the place. I need to stop." Emmaline scooted herself forward to get out of her bed. "Ugh, sorry, this baby has moved right on top of my bladder. I have peed about twenty times today and I have to go again. I'm sorry, please keep talking."

Emmaline walked out of her room to the bathroom across the hall. "I'm going to put you on speaker while I pee. Do you mind?"

"Mind. How is it any different than when you pee in front of me when we're together?" They both laughed. Emmaline had noticed recently how she was moving differently to accommodate for her growing belly. She had to adjust her stomach to sit down. Josie continued to talk about pacifiers and strollers while Emmaline finished peeing. She reached for the toilet paper and began to wipe herself. As she pulled the toilet paper out after the first swipe she gazed at the wad of soft tissues in her hand. It had blood on it.

"Oh my god, oh my god, oh my god. Josie, I'm bleeding." Josie's voice stopped at mid-sentence.

"Wait, what? Did you say bleeding?"

Emmaline stared at the wad of paper in her hands and then wiped again. More blood. Her heart pounded in her chest. Tears fell from her eyes. "Yes, there's blood. Oh my god, Josie, am I having a miscarriage?"

"Don't jump to any conclusions. Is your mom home? If she is, yell for her now."

"Mom," she yelled. "Mom!" she screamed louder.

"I'm coming. What is it? Are you okay?" Emmaline heard her mother moving down the hallway as fast as her arthritic knees would allow her. Dottie came charging into the bathroom, slamming the door open. "What's going on?" Her mother saw the blood-soaked toilet paper in Emmaline's hand. Dottie went into fight or flight mode. She unraveled a godly amount of toilet paper around her own hand and handed it to Emmaline. "Stick this in your underwear and wash your hands. We're going to the hospital."

Emmaline followed her mother's instructions without saying a word. "Dottie," came Josie's voice through the cell phone which had been placed next to the sink. "Dottie, it's Josie. I'll meet you there."

"Good. Call Jay and Andrea. They can meet us there too."

"No," came Emmaline's words a bit harshly. "No. I don't want to tell Jay until I know what is going on."

"Emmaline," came Josie's voice. "Communication, remember? He should know."

"He will. I don't want him rushing to the hospital until we know what's going on. All the lights, loud sounds, and beeping coupled with the stress of worry would instigate a migraine and I don't want to put him through that if we don't have to." Emmaline finished drying her hands, turned to her mother. They both stared at each other with fear in their eyes.

"Let's go." Emmaline ended the call with Josie and followed her mother down the hallway.

~

Emmaline was hooked up to different machines with sticky pads attached to her chest and her belly. The nurse said they were there to monitor her heartbeat and the baby's. She had an ultrasound and was waiting for the doctor on call to come in and talk to her. She took comfort in hearing her baby's heartbeat. It sounded strong. Dottie sat in a chair next to the bed fidgeting with her purse strap.

"What is taking so long?" Josie was pacing back and forth at the end of the bed.

"Jos, can you please sit down? Watching you pace is making me more nervous." Emmaline nodded toward the other empty chair in the room.

"Sorry," she said and sat down, her legs bobbing up and down nervously.

The on-call obstetrician from her doctor's office walked through the curtain carrying an iPad. A nurse followed behind her with the ultrasound machine. Emmaline glanced over at her mother and then Josie with fear in her eyes.

"Hello Emmaline, I'm Dr. Sahakyan, one of the doctors in your OB group. How are you feeling tonight?"

"Scared and worried, if I'm being honest." Emmaline's hands were shaking on her rounded belly.

"No need. Your baby is fine." Dr. Sahakyan gave Emmaline's shaking hands a gentle pat. "I'm glad you came in. Some spotting is normal during pregnancy. I want to show you what is causing your bleeding." The nurse hooked up the ultrasound machine then after squirting jelly onto the wand she handed it to the doctor. Emmaline lifted up her hospital gown exposing her pregnant belly.

Dr. Sahakyan moved the wand over Emmaline's belly and stopped at one spot. "See this here. This is your placenta. Right now, it is blocking your cervix which is causing the bleeding. This is a condition called placenta previa." Emmaline looked up at the doctor for more explanation.

"The placenta stretches and grows throughout pregnancy. It's common for it to be low in your uterus early in the pregnancy. By the time you reach your third trimester, the placenta should move to the top of your uterus. This way your baby has a clear path to the vagina for delivery."

Dottie stood up and moved closer to the monitor, worry on her face. "What if the placenta doesn't move?"

"If it doesn't move to the top of her uterus then we would schedule a C-section." The doctor smeared more jelly on Emmaline's belly moving the wand over it. Suddenly, the form of a baby took shape. The eyes, lips and one ear could be seen along with the shadowy outline of the rest of the body, hands, legs, feet, and toes. A silhouette of the life growing inside of Emmaline.

"Oh my." Dottie's hand moved to her heart in disbelief. The doctor turned the sound on. They all could hear the baby's heartbeat thumping rhythmically loud and strong. "There's my grandbaby. Hello, beautiful." Tears welled in not only Dottie's eyes, but Josie and Emmaline's as well.

"Your baby is perfectly healthy," the doctor said with a smile.

"Holy shit, Em. You have a human being growing inside of you," Josie moved closer to the monitor to get a better view. She then reached over and placed her hand on Emmaline's belly getting the gooey gel all over her palm. Suddenly, a foot kicked up on the monitor. Josie yelped and jumped back. "Holy shit, it kicked my hand. Did you see that? It felt my hand and kicked me."

They all laughed at Josie's reaction. Emmaline was relieved to know her baby was fine. She still didn't quite understand what having placenta previa meant for her pregnancy. "Dr. Sahakyan, I'm fine with having a C-section if it is what is best for the baby. I guess what I'm wondering is if there is anything I can do, or will the placenta move on its own?"

The doctor handed the wand back to the nurse who unhooked the machine and wheeled it out of the room. Dr. Sahakyan turned to the three of them. "The goal is to get you as close to your due date as possible. Delivering via C-section is often the safest treatment if bleeding continues. The position of the placenta can change as your uterus expands to accommodate your growing baby. There would have been less of a chance the placenta would move if we had discovered this later in your pregnancy. At this point we will monitor you and have you come in for more frequent prenatal appointments and ultrasounds. My recommendation is to avoid strenuous activities like running or heavy lifting, rest when you can and no sexual intercourse as it may cause bleeding. I also want to keep an eye on your blood pressure. It was a bit high today. Which may be from the events of the day, but we want to monitor that as well."

Emmaline thanked the doctor and took the towel off the bedside rail to clean the remaining gel off her belly. "Oh, one last thing before I go," the doctor said. "Do you want to know the sex of your baby?" Emmaline stared at the doctor for a moment hearing her mother catch her breath.

"Oh...um...not right now. I want to have my husband with me when we find out."

"Okay, then. I see in your chart you have another appointment scheduled in the next couple of weeks. We'll see you in the office then." They all watched the doctor turn and leave. The room fell quiet for a beat. They were all taking in everything the doctor had said and the visual memory of the tiny baby that was on the screen.

"Well, I'm going to say it again. I'm sorry, but holy shit." Josie handed Emmaline her clothes from the bag on the floor underneath the bed. "Girl, no more running for you. You are done with that. You will be resting as much as you can at work too. I'll see to that. And the sex part. Depending on you and Jay there are ways to work around intercourse to meet both of your needs."

"Josie," Emmaline said in a high-pitched tone.

"What? I'm just saying. *If* you and Jay wanted to engage, I'm sure you'd figure it out."

"Josephina Diaz, you are as bad as Vivian. Now let's get our girl home and resting." Dottie scooped up her purse and left the room to find out if they were okay to leave.

"Em, you have to tell Jay."

"I know. I'm nervous. I don't know why. It's Jay, but it's not Jay. With his mood swings and migraines, I don't know how he will react. I don't want to put any more stress and worry on him."

"I really don't think it's up to you to decide. He is the father, and he has every right to know what is going on with his wife and baby. You have two weeks before your next appointment to tell him."

Emmaline nodded in agreement with her friend.

"By the way, do you want a gender reveal party?" Josie inquired with a smirk on her face.

"Oh hell no. Stupidest thing ever started. But you are more than welcome to throw me a baby shower. Oh, let's have it at the nursing home. The residents will love it. We can play 'baby shower bingo'." Excitement emanated from Emmaline's face. In two more weeks, she would be able to say, 'my baby boy' or 'my baby girl.' She had to figure out how to tell Jay about her condition and invite him to the appointment.

CHAPTER TWENTY-FIVE

Jay

Jay had a nice visit with his mom. They took walks in the woods together, she visited with her old friends, and she sat next to him when he called Dr. Jim's office to schedule his appointment. Jay dropped her off at Bradley International Airport on Sunday afternoon. He promised he would call her after his appointment. She promised she would text and call him repeatedly if he didn't.

Monday morning, after a cup of decaf coffee, Jay took Jake out for a walk on the trails behind the house he had spent so many hours running on. He needed the fresh air to clear his mind before he went into the clinic. He knew he needed to be in a good headspace to prepare himself for the work ahead. As the fresh air blew on his face and the sound of leaves crunched under his feet, he felt a blanket of peace wash over him. Nature was healing and for the first time, he felt like he was going to be all right.

He drove to the Hospital for Special Care on Corbin Avenue in New Britain anxiety building up as his GPS brought him closer to his location. Once there he found a spot in the parking garage and sat for a few moments with the car idling. Slowly Jay bowed his head and closed his eyes. He gave himself a pep talk.

For my wife, for our baby, for our future. Then he turned off the car, pulled the key out of the ignition and opened the door. It was time for his recovery to begin.

As he walked through the double sliding glass doors, Jay saw Dr. Jim standing at the reception desk as if he had been waiting for him to arrive. Jay walked over to the tall silver-haired gentleman. Dr. Jim put his hand on Jay's back and guided him toward the elevators.

"Nervous?" asked Dr. Jim.

"A bit," he replied.

"We'll take care of you, son." Jay felt the reassurance from this father figure of a man, and it was exactly what he needed in that moment.

After his therapy appointment, Jay sat in his truck reflecting on the work he had done. He was overwhelmed by information and yet he felt better. He felt more in control of his own life. Dr. Jim had helped Jay check-in and then walked him to the office of the therapist he would be working with, Heather Preston. Surprisingly, Jay found Heather easy to talk to. He told her all about the accident, making eye contact at that last moment before the crash with Cecelia and all of the thoughts that had been going through his head over the past months.

"Do you feel guilty at all Jay?"

He was surprised at her question.

He wondered. *How did she know?*

"Yes." He put his head down and closed his eyes. The image of the ambulance pulling away with Cecelia's body in it flashed through his memory. Heather explained survivor guilt. As she spoke, he felt like she was describing all the thoughts he had those first months after the accident. To have someone say it was natural to feel the way he did was comforting on one level and not on another. He was still alive, Cecelia was not.

He spoke to her about his Bruce Banner/Incredible Hulk persona. He shared the changes he saw in himself. His frustration with his inability to recall how to do simple daily activities or to access information in his brain he knew was there, like which drawer the silverware in his own kitchen was kept or the day he couldn't remember the direction to drive to his own house.

"I can only imagine how disorienting this has all been for you. We will help you, Jay. You may not return one hundred percent to your former self, but the team here can help you learn to manage and live with your symptoms. You will learn to recognize your triggers, plan ahead for situations that might be trigging for you and teach you the skills you need to cope with them. That's what we are here for. There is no expiration date on your treatment. We are here to support you through this whenever you need us, for as long as you need us."

Heather walked him around to meet the team of therapists he would be working with. He answered their questions and explained to them the physical limitations he was experiencing since the accident, like how his gait would be off when walking and his struggle walking up and down stairs. He also told them about his inability to run and how it took him a while to feel comfortable with his balance to even walk on the trails in his woods. They all reassured him everything he was going through was normal. All of it a part of having a TBI and they were there to support him through the process of healing. He even felt a little more comfortable about the idea of taking medication for the migraines. He took a script from Dr. Jim who told him, "You have it for whenever you are ready. I promise you it is not addictive."

As Jay sat in his truck, he reflected on the past four and a half months. The time with their friends, his lack of being able to recall answers to the trivia questions. The onset of the frustration in himself, the agitation which had turned to anger, and then the anger turned to him pushing Emily and her falling down the stairs.

He took his phone out of his front pocket, opened his message app, clicked on her name, and began typing.

> **Jay:** I can't apologize enough for what happened on Christmas Eve. I am so ashamed by what I did. I don't think I can ever forgive myself. But I hope you will be able to. I started therapy this morning with Jim and his team. We even talked about medication for my migraines. I have the prescription and will be getting it filled. I'm going to make this right. I promise. I love you. Please, don't give up on us.

He read the message back to himself then hit the send button before he could change his mind. He hoped that one moment in time would not ruin the rest of their lives together. He watched as three dots appeared.

> **Emmaline:** I'm proud of you. I have a doctor's appointment in two weeks. They will be doing an ultrasound. You'll be able to see the baby and hear its heartbeat. We can find out the sex of the baby if we want. I would really like you to be there with me.

Jay's heart jumped with joy in his chest. Their baby. He would be able to see and hear their baby. Jay grinned from ear to ear. Today was what he needed. He needed hope. Between the team he met with this morning and Emmaline's text he finally felt hope. Before his mother left, he had told her he was feeling hopeless and Andrea had said to him, "Hope is something you work for." He was ready to work for it.

Jay: Of course, I will be there.

───⌖───

Jay was filled with excitement, when he got back to the cabin he decided to take the bike out for a ride. It was a seasonably warm day, he changed into a few layers of clothing, did some stretching, grabbed his helmet, and walked the bike out the front door. Before putting his helmet on his head, he breathed in the fresh, crisp air. The day seemed to keep getting better.

Jay started out slow as it had been a while since he had done any type of strenuous exercise. Once out on the main road, his body took over and he began peddling faster. It was like his body had been deprived of food for a long time and Jay was finally feeding it. The more he exerted himself, the happier he became. As he was approaching his first four-way intersection the excitement shifted to fear. He heard a car coming up from behind him. Jay became anxious and moved the handlebars too fast. The front tire hit the curb. He and the bike came crashing down onto the grassy area between the curb and the sidewalk. The passenger side window of the car that had pulled up to the stop sign rolled down, "Hey, are you all right?" The voice came from the driver's side. It was middle-aged man Jay recognized, but did not know his name.

"Yeah, I'm fine. I tried to move closer to the curb, but I guess I misjudged and moved a little too close." Jay tried to laugh it off to this stranger, but his insides were shaking with fear, images of the day of the accident flashed through his mind. The moment of impact.

"You know the entrance to the bike trail isn't far from here. It's probably nice and clear since we haven't had a real snowfall yet. You might want to think of riding there. It would be safer," the driver replied.

"Good idea. Thanks." The driver gave a nod of his head, rolled up his electric window, and drove on since there was a car behind him waiting. Jay was angry with himself. Angry he overreacted when the car approached from behind. There was plenty of space for both of them. He didn't like the anxiety that overcame him when he heard the approach of the car. Fear filled his body when he thought the car was going to hit him. Then he turned the handlebars too fast and ran into the curb. He was pissed off at himself. He could sense the anger rising like lava in a volcano bubbling up. He wanted to pick the bike up and throw it or smash it on the ground. He slowly stood up trying to calm himself down. Picking the bike up he let out a scream of frustration. It helped a little. He turned the bike around, boarded it and rode back to the cabin at a slow pace. He was overtly aware of his surroundings on his way back. A hint of fear was still pounding in his heart. *The bike trail, why didn't I think of the bike trail?* He cursed himself out. The Farmington River Trail near him was over eight miles long one way. He could easily put the bike in the back of his truck and drive to the closest parking lot.

Once he was home and settled, he felt calmer. Jay sat on the leather sofa reflected on the day. "Jake, overall, it was good day buddy. Therapy, texting with Em, the bike ride. A little mishap, but I recovered and know better for next time. I still need to work on my anger. What do you think, boy?" Jay looked down at the dog lying at his feet. Jake's rich, brown eyes met Jay's with expectancy. "Yeah, I think so to. We're getting our life back. It's going to happen." Jake lifted his head, his tongue panting in agreement.

Jay pulled out his cell phone and texted Scottie.

Jay: Took the bike out for a ride today.

Scottie: How'd it go.

Jay: Felt good until I crashed.

Scottie: What? Are you okay?

Jay: Yeah, I hugged the curb too close, hit the front tire and fell. I wanted to say thanks again for the bike. I figure at some point I'll stop by and thank everyone in person.

Scottie: They'd love to see you. Maybe we can ride together when the weather gets warmer.

Jay: Definitely

Jay looked around the living space of the cabin. It was so cozy in the winter in this room. Jay missed Emmaline being with him, snuggled up by the fire. He glanced over at the Christmas tree he had yet to take down. *This time next year, we will all be together. Em, me, and our baby. Even if it means going on the medication Dr. Jim prescribed.* He made a promise to himself. He wondered if it would help with his anxiety and mood swings as well. He needed to ask that question the next time he went to therapy. He found it interesting how he resisted going for almost five months and now he was eager to go back. After getting a drink of water, he walked over to the tree. It was a reminder of the horrible night he let his anger go too far. It was time to put it away.

The next day Jay had therapy again with Heather. He filled her in on the crash on his bike ride the previous day and the text from Emmaline. "Let's start with the text from Emmaline. She invited you to her doctor's appointment to find out the sex of the baby. How did it make you feel after reading it?"

Jay sat reflecting for a moment. "Hopeful."

"Good. And then tell me about the crash on your bike."

"I was a little apprehensive at first. It's been a while since I've been able to do any physical activity. I loved running. It was my morning ritual, it helped me get into a good mindset for the day, it was my way of relieving stress."

"What I'm hearing you say is running helped you physically and mentally." Heather sat up in her chair allowing the air to sit quietly, which encouraged Jay to elaborate more.

"Exactly. I'd start my day with a run. If I had a difficult day at work, I might come home and take Jake out for a short trail run to help get my frustration out. Since the accident, I've been agitated easily. I am frustrated with myself. My inability to do things. What was my outlet was taken away. When I was trying to run, the impact would give me migraines. Like someone was hammering a nail into my skull. Then it would turn into light sensitivity, sometimes sounds would be too much or vice versa. I would get nauseous. I also had trouble with my gait, landing my feet right without losing my balance. Without running, my release is gone. Running is another part of my identity I feel like I've lost."

"Are there other things you feel you've lost since the car accident?"

"Hell, yes. Myself. My job, my identity. Obviously, I'm worried I may be losing my wife. I see myself in the mirror sometimes and wonder who I am."

"Tell me what's different."

"I loved people, to be social. We would meet friends for trivia night every Tuesday at Mountain Laurel Brewing. I can admit I was the loudest one in the crowd. Em and I would go to baseball games either locally or travel to Boston. Road races and BBQs. Potluck dinners with friends. I love a good neighborhood block party. At work, I'd walk in and announce my arrival saying hello to everyone I walked by," Jay laughed at himself, at how over the top he could be. "I was the life of the party," he said with pride.

"How about Emmaline?"

"Em's quieter. She likes things simpler. We are both caretakers in different ways. I rush into the fire and save everyone, while she's sitting by your bedside placing a cool cloth on your forehead. We balanced each other out in that way."

"And how do you feel about yourself now?"

"Bright lights and too much noise overstimulate me and give me headaches which can lead to those intense migraines. I want things to be simpler now, quieter. I also get frustrated with myself when I can't recall things. My mood swings are so drastic. I hate myself sometimes. I hate it when I take it out on the people around me, especially Emmaline. The anger building up inside scares me. I don't know how to control it."

"We will work on the anger, but let's go back to yesterday now. Tell me about the bike ride. How it felt before you crashed, how you felt during, and then after."

Jay shifted on the small, olive-green pleather couch he was sitting on. He shared with Heather the joy he felt peddling the bike, the speed, the chilly wind on his face, the physical exertion of his body causing him to break a sweat. The anxiety which overtook him as he was approaching the four-way intersection, the stop sign and how he heard the car approaching from behind, breaking out into a cold sweat. Then he told her about the anger, the heat he felt rise from the depths of his belly. How he wanted to smash the bike. Hulk smash. Referring back to his Bruce Banner/Incredible Hulk analogy.

Heather sat and listened. Jay felt such relief to be able to voice all the things he had going on in his head. "By the time I got home, I was better. I was back to Jay Ellis/Bruce Banner. It's in those moments, I don't know what to do. If I wasn't at a four-way intersection, I probably would have smashed the bike. There were cars and people around me. I forced myself to pull it together."

"Isn't that a coping skill? You recognized the rage within yourself, and you were able to take a moment to calm yourself down. You did it all on your own. Now imagine, your inner self is holding a toolbox and inside that toolbox are all the tools you need to help you succeed in life. The pause you took was a tool you pulled out and used in the moment when you needed it. You are relearning how to deal with big emotions like you did when you were a little kid. You didn't throw yourself on the ground and have a tantrum. You took the pause to gather yourself and put yourself in a better mindset without even realizing you were doing it. That's great, Jay."

Jay looked across the desk at Heather. He hadn't even realized what he did until she pointed it out. He calmed the beast inside himself.

"Our time is about up. I'm going to give you some homework. I want you to get yourself a journal if you don't have one at home. Every time an emotion comes over you, no matter how big or small, write it down. Write down the scenario, the emotion you felt and how you handled it. Then we can come up with some strategies for ways to help you handle situations you struggled with on your own." Heather was writing on a pad of paper as she talked to Jay about his homework. She ripped the sheet of paper from its pad and handed it to Jay. "Here you go. Here's your homework. I'll see you next week."

Jay took the paper from her hand and read what Heather wrote.

Homework assignment: it can be bullet points if easier.
- scenario
- emotion
- outcome

Jay read through it a couple of times matching the words to what happened the day before. First the scenario, emotions, and outcome from texting with Emmaline and then the bike ride. He found it interesting to designate them into those three categories. *Guess I'm hitting the store on the way home to buy myself a journal.*

CHAPTER TWENTY-SIX

Emmaline

Emmaline was glad Jay had texted her on Sunday. One because he had texted to say he was finally going to therapy and two because she was able to text him about her next doctor's appointment. She knew she needed to tell him about her placenta previa. She didn't know why she was avoiding it as the doctor said it was something they needed to monitor. They were in a wait and see stage. She needed to take better care of herself. When she thought of telling him in person different scenarios played out in her head. She worried he would worry, and it would add additional stress onto his recovery. She was afraid he would be mad she hadn't moved back home where he could take care of her and the baby. She knew she should go home. They should be experiencing her pregnancy together.

She feared his anger could erupt at any moment, putting her or the baby in harm's way. Her childhood trauma from her father had been creeping back up in her since the first time Jay yelled at her after the accident. Then when he shoved her and pushed her down the stairs, it brought back all the memories of the times her father had hit her and her mother. She never thought Jay was like her father. At least the man she married was not. This Jay, she didn't know.

"Emmaline!" Her mother came racing through the automatic double doors of the nursing home. Em was sitting at the front desk finishing up paperwork from the day. She glanced over at the top of the desk and saw the scared expression on her mother's face.

"Mom, what's the matter? What happened?" Emmaline stood up and rushed around to the front of the desk.

"She's bad, Em. She's in a really bad state today. I need your help getting her out of the car." Emmaline saw her mother holding her left arm close to her body.

"What happened to your arm?" Emmaline followed her mother back out the double doors to the car parked at the front entrance.

"I noticed Viv was not herself when I picked her up after breakfast. I couldn't put my finger on it, but she was acting odd. Odder than her usual odd. We were preparing the dough for the bread order for this week. Everything was fine. We were in our usual groove. Then she started mumbling to herself. Again, I didn't think much of it. She mumbles or sings to herself all the time. But her tone was harsher, her face angrier. That's when she came at me with a rolling pin."

They reached the passenger side door. Emmaline could see her aunt through the window. She was definitely angry about something. Em opened the door. "Mother fuckers. Let me out of here. You can't do this to me. Who the hell do you think you are?" Viv turned and glared at Emmaline. "Who the fuck are you? Where are you taking me?"

"Aunt Viv, it's Emmaline, your niece. I'm taking you to your room. Here let me help you out of your seatbelt." Emmaline reached around to unbuckle Viv, instead she got a backhand to the face.

"Don't you fucking touch me, girlie."

Emmaline stepped back in shock. Vivian unbuckled her seatbelt and got out of the car. Emmaline glanced over at her mother. They were both wearing the same expressions on their faces. Shock.

"I won't touch you. I promise." Emmaline had been working with dementia patients long enough to have seen the irritated and violent side of them. Luckily for her, Viv's backhand slap only grazed across the top of her head as Emmaline was bent over.

Emmaline walked next to Viv at a cautious distance using a soft, soothing voice as she spoke. "You must be tired. Seems like you've had a long day. Would you like me to run you a bath and turn your bed down for you?"

"I am tired actually. A hot bath would be lovely." Dottie and Emmaline followed Viv into the building and down the hall. Emmaline caught the eye of her nurse supervisor, Maggie, who was standing at the nurses' station as they walked by. She mouthed; *she needs her meds*. The supervisor nodded in understanding.

It took about an hour to get Viv settled into her bed. After a bath, her meds and a cup of tea Vivian appeared to be calmer. More like herself. Dottie was visibly shaken up from the day. Emmaline led her mother to the front sitting room. "Let me take a look at your arm." Emmaline reached out and gently took her mother's arm in her hands. Dottie winced when Emmaline tried to turn her wrist over. "It doesn't appear to be broken; it is really swollen though. You might want to have it checked out. In the meantime, I can wrap it up in an ACE bandage. Are you okay?"

Emmaline still held her mother's arm and hand gently in her own. "She really scared me today. I've never seen her in a state like that. I'm going to make an appointment tomorrow with her doctor. See if we can get her meds adjusted or increased."

"That's a good idea." Emmaline got up and walked away. Minutes later she came with a bandage for her wrist. "Is there anything I can do for you, Mom? Do you need help with the bread."

Dottie's head dropped. "I completely forgot about the bread orders. How am I going to make bread with my wrist like this?" Dottie accentuated the question by raising her left forearm in the air. "I'll call Perino's tomorrow and cancel the bread orders for this week. I hate to do it, but I have no other choice. You should see the kitchen. It's a complete mess. It will take me forever to clean it up."

"Don't worry, mom. I can help you when I get home."

"No, you can't. Remember no strenuous activities. Would you be okay with me calling Jay and asking if he could help me? I have that large bag of flour which is now half spilt on the floor. The mixers sitting there with half-mixed ingredients. I think some muscle would make clean up go faster." Emmaline thought about it for a second. If she were back at the cabin and her mother had called her to tell her about this situation, Jay would have jumped up and driven right over without having to be asked. It was the type of guy he is/was.

"I think you should call Jay. Actually, I'll text him right now. By the time you get home, he'll probably be pulling into the driveway." She gave her mother a hug and walked her back out to her car.

On her walk back to the building, she pulled her cell phone out of her pink scrubs pocket.

> **Emmaline:** Viv had a bad day with Mom. Mom dropped her off. She needs help with cleaning up the mess Viv made at the house. Would you be able to go over and help her? Maybe bring the shop vac. I'm still at work.

Within seconds three dots appeared and then a text.

Jay: You bet. Heading over now.

He is still that guy, Emmaline thought with a smile on her face.

CHAPTER TWENTY-SEVEN

Jay

Dottie pulled into the driveway right after Jay arrived. Jay watched her get out of the car and walk over to his truck. He got out and walked to meet her. "I hear you had a fun day with Viv, eh?"

"Fun is definitely not what I would call it. I've never seen her behave this way. Viv is a SOB but not a mean one. I've never seen her like this, Jay. She really scared me and injured me." She held up her wrapped wrist for emphasis.

"What happened?" Jay asked as he grabbed the shop vac out of the back of his truck and followed Dottie into the house.

"I honestly don't know. One minute she's rolling out dough, the next she screaming incoherently and chasing me around the kitchen with a rolling pin trying to hit me over the head with it. I used my arm to block her, she got me good on my wrist several times. I was finally able to rip the rolling pin out of her hand. Not sure if the wrist injury is from the whacks of the rolling pin or me pulling it out of her hands. Em took a look at it. She wrapped it but thinks I should still see a doctor." Dottie led Jay through the front door, across the living room and into the kitchen. She flicked the light on.

"Wow! Um...yeah, I'm glad you called me." Jay scanned the kitchen. Three Cuisinart mixers were covered in splattered dough with the remnants from the bowls contents sprayed all over the counter, backsplash, and floor. A fifty-pound bag of flour had been tipped over. There was flour dusting across the kitchen island spilling down onto the floor. Balls of bread dough and half rolled out dough sitting in clumps hardening in the air on the countertop. "Dottie, go take care of yourself. I got this."

"No, Jay, I couldn't. I'll help. It's my mess."

"I insist. Get some ice for your wrist and go relax. It won't take me long." Jay saw a grateful smile crossover Dottie's face. He plugged in the shop vac and began making his way around the floor cleaning up the dough splatters and spilt flour first, so he didn't slip on any of it.

Jay was so focused on his cleanup project he didn't see Emmaline standing in the doorway of the kitchen. It was the first time he'd seen her since she told him she was pregnant on Christmas Day. He stopped cold when he met her eyes. She was smiling the sweetest smile at him. It made his heart leap. He glanced down at her stomach. She had the cutest little baby bump. She was the most beautiful thing he had ever seen. Her light brown hair pulled into a messy ponytail, no makeup and her pregnant belly popping out from her scrub shirt. He wanted to run across the kitchen and wrap her in his arms. "Hey," he said shyly.

"Hi," she said in return. Emmaline peered down at her belly a bit self-consciously. "Thanks for coming over to help."

"Of course," He waited for her eyes to meet his. He couldn't hold it in. "You're beautiful."

He watched her shift around uncomfortably. She was never good at taking a compliment. "Um...thank you. Do you need help?"

"Nah, I'm almost done. How's Viv doing?"

"Better. Maggie gave her a sedative to help calm her down. I helped her with dinner and got her into bed before I left. I'm not going to sugar coat it. It was rough. I understand why Mom was frightened by her behavior. It took us quite a bit of time to get her settled. She called me words I didn't even know existed or could be combined together to be an insult."

Jay laughed. He could only imagine what must have come out of Viv's mouth. Truckers would never be able to hold a candle to a vulgar word off with Vivian. "You must be tired."

"That's an understatement. My feet are killing me. Since my belly popped, I'm feeling the extra weight of the baby in my feet and my low back. Trust me, I'm not complaining. Takes a little bit of time to get used to it."

"Are you able to take breaks and get off of your feet if you need to?"

"When Josie and I are on the same shift, I have no choice. She yells at me." Emmaline laughed. Jay loved the sound of her laugh. He loved how they were having a normal conversation.

"Is there anything I can do for you?" Jay had so many other questions he wanted to ask her that had been going round and round in his head like a Ferris wheel. *Are we okay? Are you coming home? What's happening with us? Have you left me for good? How can I convince you I'm not going to be like your dad?* He didn't want to ask any of them at that moment. He wanted to enjoy being in her presence. Soaking her up and talking about her pregnancy, their baby.

"I'm okay. Thank you. If you don't need any help and if you don't mind, I think I'm going to take a hot bath and soak the day away."

"Of course. Go ahead. Take care of yourself. I'm almost done here and then I'll be heading out." Emmaline paused at the door. It felt to Jay like she had more to say but was holding back.

He waited expectantly. They held eye contact for an extra-long moment, then Emmaline turned and walked away.

Jay let out a breath. *What did she want to say?* He wondered. His heart ached for her. He knew he needed to be patient. Heather told him in his last session it would be good to invite Emmaline to one of their appointments. She said it might be easier to talk in a neutral setting with someone else there as a buffer. He wanted to ask Emmaline if she would come to therapy with him and he didn't know how to bring it up. He was hoping he could mention it when he went to the ultrasound appointment with her. He hoped the baby would be what brings them back together.

Emmaline

Emmaline lay in the bathtub staring down at her tiny baby bump. She gently caressed her belly like she was making circles on her unborn baby's back. She was thinking about Jay in the kitchen, watching his strong arms and tall physique while he put the baking supplies away. She missed him terribly. She missed them together and she knew she was the one keeping them apart. Suddenly, Emmaline felt movement, a flutter. She sat up taller in the tub. *Is that what I think it is?*

"Jay," she spoke. She felt another movement. "Jay," she said louder. She heard Jay's footsteps running down the hallway of her mother's ranch. Jay entered the bathroom to find her lying naked in a tub of water, her face frozen in shock. At that moment, she didn't care that she was completely exposed.

"Is ev—" He didn't have a chance to finish his sentence before Emmaline reached out, grabbed his hand, and pulled it down onto her belly. He almost slipped and fell on the fluffy, white bathmat as he dropped down to his knees.

"Do you feel it? Can you? Can you feel the baby moving?" Emmaline continued to adjust his hand to the spot on her belly. Right at the moment his hand connected to her skin he felt a little thump, like a flick of fingers. Then there was a wave of movement under his hand.

"Oh my God, is that..." He looked up at her with questioning eyes and nodded. Tears filled his eyes. The baby moved again under their stacked hands. They both laughed. He leaned over and lightly kissed Em on her forehead and then placed another kiss on her belly where he felt the baby. His eye met hers. "I love you."

He stood and left the room. "Where are you going?" she asked calling after him.

"Heather, my therapist, said it will help me if I write down when I experience big emotions. I have to write this down. I don't want to ever forget this moment. I need to find some paper and a pen. I'll be right back."

Emmaline smiled to herself, kissed the tips of her fingers, and placed them on her belly. *I think I just fell in love with my husband all over again.*

$\operatorname{\sim}$

Jay

Jay raced into the living room where Dottie was relaxing. He powerwalked to the desk by the window, grabbing some paper and a pen from the holder. "What is going on? Is everything okay?" Dottie asked him.

"Better than okay. Amazing. I felt the baby move inside Em's belly. It kicked my hand. Like it knew I was there. I'm Daddy.

The baby knew it was me." Jay was grinning ear to ear as he walked back down the hallway while trying to frantically write all of his thoughts and feelings on the paper.

Jay stayed another hour chatting with Dottie with the television playing some game show in the background. Emmaline came in and joined them after she had changed into her pajamas. Jay could smell her scent in the air. A combination of lavender and mint.

"I'll have to call the Perino's in the morning to tell them I won't be able to fill the bread orders for a couple of weeks. I feel terrible. In all the years I worked for them I've never had to cancel an order. But how am I supposed to bake with my wrist wrapped like this." Dottie sat in the brown, leather chair staring at her wrapped wrist in her lap.

"Don't cancel. I can help." Jay shocked himself. The words came out of his mouth before he even realized it. Thinking about it for a beat, he liked the idea. He needed more to do to fill his day and liked helping Dottie.

"Really, Jay. You wouldn't mind?" Dottie asked.

"I'd love it. I need more things to do. My therapy is only three days a week. I can't sit around the house all day having a pity party for myself anymore. I need more purpose in my day. Teach me how to make bread."

"Okay. We're already behind for this week with the loss of today. Do you think you can be here early tomorrow morning? Like five a.m. early? I'll have everything ready to go by the time you get here."

"Absolutely."

"Are you sure, Jay? You don't think it will be too much for you?" Emmaline asked him with concern in her eyes.

"Not at all. I want more to do with my day. The pity party's over. I need some purpose. Dottie and I can throw on some fun music and beat some dough." "I like that plan." Dottie smiled over at him. "Okay you two. I've had enough excitement for today. I'm going to bed. Goodnight, sweetheart, and I'll see you bright and early tomorrow morning Jay." Dottie slowly stood from her chair and headed down the hall to her bedroom.

"Jay, are you sure you'll be okay with this?" Emmaline stood from her spot on the couch.

"Yes, don't worry. I'm going stir crazy in the cabin. I need more to do. I'll bring Jake too. I'm sure he'd love a change of scenery. Maybe I can even bike over some days." Jay was thinking out loud now.

"Bike?" Em looked at him with confusion on her face.

"The crew at work chipped in and got me a road bike to help with my recovery since I'm still not running. Scottie brought it over on Christmas Day." There was a bit of an awkward silence at the mention of Christmas. "I've only taken it out once. It felt good to be moving again. I want to continue while there's still no snow on the ground."

"That's fantastic, Jay. Sounds like your creating new outlets for yourself." They both walked to the front door. Jay reached for the doorknob then paused.

"I'm working on it, Em. I really am. I want you to know I'm taking my treatment seriously. I want my family back. I want you home. I miss you." He reached for her hand. They stood there holding hands both gazing down at their intertwined fingers. "My therapist suggested you join us sometime. It would mean a lot to me if you came."

"Really?" She looked up at him.

"Absolutely." He squeezed her hand gently.

"I think I'd like that." Jay leaned over and gave her a soft kiss on her cheek before he turned and left. Another step forward.

CHAPTER TWENTY-EIGHT

Jay

Jay woke up the next morning filled with a sense of overwhelming joy like he hadn't experienced in over six months. The night before gave him the hope he needed. It was four in the morning. Even though it was daybreak, he decided to get an early start over to Dottie's house. He had no idea how to bake anything. He was curious to see how the day would go.

Jay arrived at Dottie's by four thirty. She was already up and prepping. They got into a groove where Dottie explained what needed to be done and Jay followed her lead. Dottie put the Steely Dan radio station on Spotify and they both sang along to the songs as they worked. Emmaline came into the kitchen and made herself a cup of tea. She leaned against the counter watching them work.

"You're a tea drinker now?" Jay asked her, nodding his head at the mug in her hand.

"Yeah, you're not supposed to drink too much coffee when you're pregnant. I save my one cup a day for my afternoon lull. Are you a tea drinker now?" she asked while pulling the cup to her mouth for another sip.

"I am. I resisted it, but my mom made me a cup when she was here, and it was good. I even bought a variety pack to try different types of tea. English breakfast is probably my favorite." Jay watched as she turned the tag on her teabag around. It said, English Breakfast Blend. They smiled at each other.

"Okay you too. I'm off. Hoping today is a better day for Viv. Mom, Maggie said she would contact Viv's doctor today about her medication. I'll keep you posted." Emmaline put her tea bag in the garbage can and the mug into the dishwasher.

"I'd appreciate it. Please thank her for me." Dottie responded while measuring out flour into the mixing bowl. Her bandage was covered in the white powder that had drifted into the air.

"Whoa...this little one is active this morning," Emmaline placed her hand under her belly holding onto it.

"Are you okay?" Jay started to walk over to her with concern on his face.

"I'm fine. Really. I have to get to work. Have fun today." Emmaline grabbed her purse and car keys and headed out the door.

Jay and Dottie watched her leave still holding onto her lower belly. "I wish she would slow down. The doctor told her not to put so much stress on her body. She has to stop pushing herself."

"What do you mean?" Jay asked a bit confused.

"Oh...I...you know...um, never mind." Dottie waved her hand at him as if to say it was no big deal. He could see by the expression on her face it was a big deal.

"Dottie, what are you not telling me?"

Jay listened as Dottie filled him in on Emmaline's placenta previa and the suggestions the doctor had made for her. He was trying to not get visibly upset in front of Dottie. *I can't believe she didn't call me. I can't believe she didn't tell me.* Jay was trying to control his irritation as the anger began to build up in him. He quickly grabbed the notepad he had started carrying around with him from his back pocket and began writing down his feelings. He could sense Dottie's eyes glancing over at him while she continued to work. When he was done, he closed the book and put it back in his pocket. He felt better. The volcano that had started building him had settled down.

"Are you okay?" Dottie asked while she preheated the oven.

"Yes and no. I wish she had called me. I wish I was there for her. I should be there for her."

"Jay, she didn't want to worry you, and she was afraid all of the lights and sounds of the hospital would bring on a migraine for you. I know she was planning on telling you, maybe the opportunity hadn't come yet." He knew Dottie was trying to lighten things up. He would need to talk to Em about it. He wanted to be a part of her pregnancy, the good and bad.

He and Dottie continued to bake slowly getting back into their groove and singing to the music. The thought of Emmaline or the baby being at any risk made him feel sick to his stomach, but he would push it down for now. At least until he could talk to Em.

Jay heard a car pull into the driveway when he was taking the first set of bread out of the oven. It was Emmaline. He had seen her lunch box in the refrigerator when he went in to get more eggs. He assumed that must be why she had come back. He thought about her being in the emergency room the week before. His anger started to boil. He closed his eyes and took a few deep breaths, another tool he had learned in therapy.

Emmaline walked through the door; she was holding her lower belly again. "Hi," she said without meeting his eyes.

"Are you okay?" He walked over to her offering his hand.

"Yeah, I'm fine. I was really tired. Josie, being the worry wart, sent me home. I'm going to go lay down." Emmaline started to walk away from him.

"Em, Dottie told me." Emmaline turned around slowly unsure of what he meant by what he had said. "The placenta previa. She let it slip, so don't be upset with her. I wish it was you who told me. I wish you had called me so I could have been there for you."

Emmaline stood awkwardly shifting from one foot to the other. "I was planning on telling you. Things were weird between us. I didn't want to worry you. I didn't want the hospital to overstimulate you causing a migraine."

"Em, I want to know these things. You're my wife, that's my baby. I need to know if you are both okay. I want to be a part of this pregnancy with you. This is something we both wanted. We planned to have a family together. The accident may have complicated things, but it didn't change the fact that I love you and want a life with you." Jay's voice was getting higher and harsher in tone. He walked over to where Emmaline was standing and reached a hand toward her. Emmaline cowered away at his approach.

"Oh my god, Em. I am not going to hit you. I'm not going to hurt you. Why can't you believe me? I'm not your father. I can get frustrated without getting violent. I can get mad without lashing out. You need to know that. Don't make me pay for what your father did."

"I'm sorry." She started to cry as she turned and walked away from him. "I can't do this with you right now."

"Let me at least help you into bed. I can fluff some pillows or something."

"Please, Jay, not right now."

Dottie came through the basement door at that moment. "What's going on? Emmaline, what are you doing home?" Dottie's head rotated side-to-side as she glanced between the couple.

"I...um...I started bleeding again." Emmaline said the words softly.

"What?" Jay's voice echoed in the room. "Why didn't you say that when you first walked in. Should we go to the hospital? Should we call your doctor?"

"Stop yelling at me," Emmaline was crying harder as she clutched her belly and bent over.

"I'm not yelling at you. I'm concerned for you."

"Enough. Both of you. Emmaline go lay down. Jay go to the kitchen and start cleaning up. We are done for today. I will call the doctor's office and ask what we should do." Dottie fanned herself exasperated by the two of them. Jay watched Emmaline walk down the dark hallway. He turned and huffed his way back into the kitchen. He began cleaning. He couldn't believe she recoiled from his touch. Couldn't she see he was doing better? He was working on his mood swings and outbursts.

CHAPTER TWENTY-NINE

Emmaline

Emmaline laid down on her childhood bed. She couldn't believe this was happening. Why did Jay have to be here when she got home? She wanted to crawl into her bed, wrap her baby belly in her arms and fall asleep. She wanted to wake up and everything would be better. Instead, she was bleeding again, she felt her body cramping and she got into an argument with Jay. She didn't know why she flinched when he approached her. Actually, she did know, it was from all the times her father would be nice to her and a flick of a switch he would turn and start yelling at her or her mother, shove them, hit them, smack them on the side of the head. They never knew when the next blow would come. They would start to feel safe in his presence and that's when he would strike. The change in Jay since his accident had brought all of these emotions from her childhood to the surface.

Emmaline's cell phone rang from her purse on her bedside table. She was going to ignore it, but thought maybe it was the doctor's office calling her to follow up from her mother's call. She pulled out her cell phone. It was Josie. "Hello."

"Hey, you were supposed to call me when you got home."

Emmaline could hear commotion from the nursing home in the background on Josie's end.

"Sorry. I got home and Jay was here, we sort of argued, then he went to comfort me, and I backed away from him. Mom told him about my condition, he got upset because I didn't tell him. It's a whole thing. Jo, I'm really screwing everything up. He's trying. I know he is finally trying. I think I'm making it worse for us."

"First of all, stop beating yourself up. You can't put any more stress on you or the baby. And second, he knows now. It's done and over with. Jay's a good guy. Let him in. It's time to include him in on the pregnancy. Maybe you should think about going home, Em," Josie quietly added.

"I don't know." Emmaline pulled the covers up closer to her chin.

"What are you afraid of?" The noises in the background had muffled which meant Josie must have moved into the supply closet behind the desk.

Emmaline finally vocalized the fear she had been holding inside. "I'm afraid he's going to turn into my father."

"Wow, Daddy issues much. Come on, Em. Your father was bipolar with violent tendencies. Jay was in a car accident. He may be a quieter version of himself. He may get agitated more easily because he's frustrated by his limitations, but he's still the guy you married. He has a huge heart, and he loves you."

"It's not only me anymore. I have our baby to protect. I look at him and see the man I married and then I think of his behavior over the last six months and worry that this is how he will be."

"Babe, you need to give him time to heal. He witnessed the last moments of Cecelia's life, he got knocked around in the car accident, put on leave from work, had his identity stripped from him, and then you move out. The guy has had a shitty go of it. I'm not saying it's your fault in any way. I'm not saying it hasn't been tough for you too. I'm saying don't assume this is what life for the two of you will be like forever. He's going to therapy. He's getting help. It might not be a bad idea for you to do the same."

Emmaline felt her phone buzz. She pulled it away from her ear and saw another call was coming in. "Josie, I have to let you go, my doctor's office is calling."

"Keep me posted."

Emmaline switched over to the other call and talked to the nurse at her obstetrician's office. She was told to go to the hospital immediately.

The three of them drove over to the hospital in Dottie's car as it was easier for Emmaline to get in and out of her mother's Subaru. Her obstetrician's office had called ahead to let the hospital know she was coming. Once Emmaline was checked in, she was brought straight into a curtained off room. A nurse rushed through the curtain sliding the little beads attached to the track flying to the other side. "Hi, Emmaline. I'm Cynthia, I'll be your nurse." Before Emmaline had a chance to say hi in return Cynthia had taken her temperature, put a blood pressure cuff on her arm and hooked her and the baby up to monitors. Cynthia left as quickly as she came in with the same whooshing sound of the curtain moving on the tracks. "A doctor will be in shortly."

"Wow, efficient. I like her." Dottie sat in a chair next to Emmaline holding her purse on her lap. Em could tell her mother was nervous by how upright she sat and the way she clenched her bag. They could hear the pulsating sound of the baby's heartbeat on the monitor. Emmaline closed her eyes and listened. Her baby sounded okay. Emmaline glanced over at Jay. Something was wrong she could tell.

"Jay, are you okay? Do you want to sit?" Emmaline pointed to another chair right outside the curtain he could grab.

"Um...yeah. The lights are really bright and there's a lot of noise. I'm fine. Let's take care of you." Jay dragged the chair over and sat in it. She watched him put his head down and cover his ears with his hands. At that moment, Cynthia came whooshing back in with a rolling stand and an iPad attached to it.

"Emmaline, I'm going to ask you a few questions while we wait for the doctor, okay?" Cynthia was waiting for an answer from Emmaline, but she couldn't take her eyes off of Jay. Finally, she asked, "You okay over there, sir?"

Jay slowly looked up. "Yeah. My brain is a bit overstimulated. I'm trying to think of the coping skill I learned in therapy to help with my anxiety, it was something about using my senses."

The tall, thin Black woman with beautiful flowing braids knelt down in front of Jay. "Name five things you can see," she said to him, placing a calming hand on his knee.

Emmaline watched Jay scan the room with his eyes. "Fluorescent lights shining bright, baby bump under cotton gown, Emmaline's worried brow, your bright green Crocs, the cracked tile on the floor."

"Name four things you can touch."

Emmaline saw Jay stare down at his hands. "The seam of my jeans, the texture of the chair I'm sitting on." She watched him slowly stand up and move over to her, placing a hand on her belly. "My child." He moved his hand over to her hand. "My wife's delicate fingers."

Cynthia smiled at him. "Name three things you can hear."

Emmaline watched as Jay closed his eyes and listened for a moment. "The sound of our baby's heartbeat, the background noise of the hospital beyond the curtain, my breathing."

Cynthia stood up next to him. She spoke slowly, quietly, "name two things you can smell."

Emmaline took an inhale at the same time as Jay did. "Antiseptic." They all laughed. "Lavender and mint shampoo." Emmaline was taken aback. It was her shampoo. He could smell her shampoo. He knew her shampoo. She felt a flutter in her stomach, and it wasn't the baby this time.

"You're doing great. Now, name one thing you can taste." Cynthia pulled a Lifesaver mint out of her scrub pocket and handed it to Jay. He opened it and put it in his mouth.

"Mint."

"How do you feel?" Cynthia asked gently placing a hand on Jay's arm as he stood next to the hospital bed.

"Better. Thank you."

Emmaline and Dottie sat there speechlessly. Finally, Dottie spoke. "How did you know how to do that?"

Cynthia turned to Dottie and smiled, "I've been doing this a long time. I also have five kids at home. Trust me when I tell you, I've needed to do that same technique on myself many times." Cynthia turned her attention back to Emmaline. "The whole room seems much calmer now." She smiled at her.

Emmaline was grateful for Cynthia. She was also impressed at how Jay handled the situation. The curtain slid open, and a short, red-headed male doctor walked in. Emmaline spent three hours answering a million questions, waiting, being poked and prodded, waiting some more. Finally, the doctor came back in and said they would be able to go home.

"Your baby is fine. Healthy heartbeat and measurements, ultrasound was great. However, your placenta is still covering the birth canal and hasn't moved. I know this is probably not what you want to hear, but I spoke with Dr. Sahakyan, and we both agree you need to be on bed rest for the remainder of your pregnancy." Emmaline sat up a little straighter. She looked at her mom, then Jay, then back to the doctor. "Take it easy, limit your activity, avoid heavy lifting, going up and down stairs too much. You are at the twenty-week mark. We want to get you as close to your delivery date as possible and if nothing changes, we will schedule a C-section. Take this time to rest, do some light nesting, read books, catch up on streaming shows. Call Dr. Sahakyan's office tomorrow and set up an appointment if you don't have one already scheduled. They will go over your care plan for the remainder of your pregnancy in more detail." The doctor smiled at Emmaline as if he had given her good news.

Emmaline could tell the doctor was trying to make light of the situation. She couldn't imagine not working. She was saving her sick time up for after the baby arrived. She wasn't sure what this would mean for her job. Her baby was her priority, and she knew she would do whatever it took to bring her child into the world safely.

"Thank you," she said to the doctor's back as he walked out of the room. "Bed rest. Wow. What am I going to do about work? I don't know if I can take that much time off."

"Don't worry about it right now. Let's get you home and in bed," Dottie said while putting on her coat.

"What? No. I want her to come home to the cabin. I can take care of her. I can be with her. She'll be able to rest peacefully at the cabin with me and Jake." Jay stood adamantly by Emmaline's side.

"The bedrooms are upstairs, kitchen downstairs. How can she possibly stay at the cabin?"

"I'll move the guest bed down to the first floor."

"How will she shower? You don't have a full bathroom on the main floor."

"I'll carry her up the stairs."

"When she's nine months pregnant."

"I'll install a standing shower. All the hookups are there, it wouldn't take too long to get it set up for you."

. "Stop, please." Emmaline couldn't think straight with both of them bickering over the hospital bed like she was the net of their verbal tennis match. "Can we go back to Mom's house for now? She's right Jay, the ranch is better suited for bed rest than the cabin. If you want, you can come over and babysit the pregnant lady. Bring Jake too. I miss my boy."

Emmaline saw the defeated look on Jay's face, but he did not protest. They all left quietly together absorbing the events of the day.

CHAPTER THIRTY

Jay

Jay walked through the automated doors of the Hospital for Special Care the next morning with a purpose in his step. "Slow down there, son. You're in hurry to get to therapy this morning."

Jay turned and saw Dr. Jim quickening his pace to walk alongside him. "I can't even begin to tell you about everything that has happened over the last few days. It all started with Viv having a difficult day and ended with Emmaline in the hospital. She's fine. The baby's fine." Jay followed up quickly. As they were walking past the ladies' room, Heather came out of the door.

"Perfect timing. I can tell you both."

"Hello to you as well. Tell us what?" Heather fell in step with them.

Jay filled them in on what happened between Vivian and Dottie. How Dottie needed help making bread. "I really enjoy baking. I never knew that. Getting lost in the music while kneading the dough. It was quite soothing."

"That's great, Jay. It might be something for you to explore. A new hobby," Heather said as they made their way into her office.

He continued on with his story telling them how Dottie let Emmaline's condition slip, Emmaline coming home, how she flinched when he reached for her.

"Did she say why she didn't tell you about her condition?" Dr. Jim sat on the corner of Heather's desk while Jay sat in his usual spot on the small sofa. Heather walked behind the desk to her leather chair.

"She was afraid it would upset me, she didn't want to worry me, she was waiting for the right time, she knew I was going with her to her next ultrasound. I don't know. The fact is when I got upset because I was worried about her and the baby, she thought I was mad and cowered away from me. She thinks I'm going to hit her. I don't know how to get it through her head, I'm not her father. I'm not going to hurt her." Jay was getting himself worked up. He closed his eyes and took several deep breaths before continuing.

"Maybe Emmaline needs to go see her father. It might help her resolve some of these issues." Heather glanced up at Dr. Jim and then at Jay. He saw a non-verbal exchange between the two of them. He couldn't quite figure out what it meant.

"She hasn't seen or spoken to her father since she was twelve years old. I don't know if anyone knows if he's alive or where he is."

"Jim, I'm sure you could help them out with that." Heather kept her gaze on Jim.

"Confidentiality, Heather," Dr. Jim said firmly.

"It would be good for all of their healing."

"What are you both talking about?" Jay shifted his eyes from one to the other not quite sure he understood what was happening. "Do you know where Emmaline's father is?"

Dr. Jim coughed into his fist. "All I will say is, her father was a patient of mine. Dottie came to me after she kicked him out."

"What did she want?" Jay asked him confused.

"She wanted me to know she had thrown him out and asked if I could keep an eye on him. He had been a patient of mine off and on for a while. Raymond had a tough time accepting his mental illness. After Dottie kicked him out, he came to me ready for help. He was a patient here for a long time. I still manage his medication."

"That means he's still around. He's in the area. Does Dottie know?" Jay was mind blown. He couldn't process this new information.

"I think it's best if you talk to Dottie about this. Again, patient confidentiality. I've said enough. Probably too much. Now fill us in on the rest of what happened. You haven't told us how Em ended up in the hospital."

Jay appreciated Dr. Jim's concern for Emmaline. He continued with his story. He told them how Emmaline came home from work because of her bleeding, the trip to the hospital, how Cynthia helped him with the five senses coping skill. He shared what the doctor said about Emmaline needing to be on bed rest. "I want her to move home. I want to be there for her and the baby. Dottie's house is a one-floor ranch while the cabin is two floors with the bedroom and full bathroom upstairs. The doctor said she should avoid stairs. I know it makes sense for her to stay at her mom's, but I want her home with me. I want to take care of her."

"I'm proud of you, Jay. The hospital is a place which could have led to a migraine for you. You stayed and used a coping skill because you wanted to be there for your wife. That's a great step forward." Heather was beaming at Jay. He hadn't realized until she pointed out how successfully he had handled the situation. He smiled.

"She's right, Jay. It's another step forward. All the skills you're learning here are great, but it's applying them to real life situations which will make the healing process better for you."

Dr. Jim stood up and patted Jay on the shoulder. "Well, I've got patients to see. I better get going. I'm sorry for what you and Emmaline are going through, but sometimes these things can be blessings in disguise."

"I hope so."

"And hope is worth fighting for." Jim said as he walked out the door. Jay's head shot up. Jim had said the exact words his mother had said to him.

"I couldn't agree with him more. This difficult situation could be what begins to bring you both back together. Try dating each other."

Jay was confused. He was not sure he understood what Heather meant. "Date each other?"

"Yes, date each other. Get to know each other again. She's on bed rest. Take her to the movies."

"She's on bed rest. How am I supposed to take her to the movies?"

"Oh Jay, use your imagination. Her mom's house has a television. I'm sure Dottie has a microwave too. Pop some popcorn, crawl in bed next to her and watch a movie. She's going to have to leave the house for appointments with the doctor. Take her and then go somewhere. Make it a date. Be romantic. Woo your wife. If she's open to it, she's welcome to come to an appointment with you."

Jay liked the idea. Date Emmaline. More small steps. Build her trust again. "I'm going to do it. I'm going to date my wife." Jay was grinning ear to ear. Heather laughed at him. Jay stood up, reached his hand across the desk, and shook Heather's hand as if they were sealing a deal they had just made. He walked out with a lighter step at the prospect of spending more time with Emmaline.

On the drive home, Jay reflected on the conversation about Emmaline's father. *I can't believe he is local. I can't believe Dottie knows and never said anything to Em about him.* Jay couldn't wait to get home to his computer. It was time for him to brush the cobwebs off his police skills and do some investigating. Once he was settled back in at the cabin, Jay pulled up Google and searched Raymond Jacobs New Britain, CT. Raymond Jacobs was a more common name than he anticipated. He scrolled through a few rabbit holes until he came up with a few names that fit. Based on age, occupation, and years in the city he narrowed it down to two likely Raymond Jacobs. He wrote down the addresses of both men and closed the laptop's cover. *Time to go find Mr. Jacobs.*

Jay felt like he was spending most of the day driving around in his truck. It felt good, like when he drove around in his patrol car. He liked this sense of purpose coursing through his veins. He missed it. He was so distracted with the mission he was on he didn't feel the anxiety he had felt on previous trips while driving in his truck. The first address brought him to a four-story, red, brick apartment building. He drove around the neighborhood. He parked the truck. He sat there for about fifteen minutes waiting to see if anyone went in or came out. There was no activity. He decided to go up to the front door and check the names next to the buzzers to make sure Raymond Jacobs still lived there. His heartbeat faster as he crossed the street and up the walkway to the door. It was a nice building, well maintained landscaping, the backs of air conditioner units hanging out of windows. He scanned the names. R. Jacobs – 22C. *He's still here.*

Jay went back to his truck and drove to the next address. The house was located down a tree-lined street with sidewalks. There were old colonial houses up and down both sides of the street.

The homes were well kept by their owners. He looked at the numbers on the mailbox until he got to 508. It was a white colonial with black shutters and a short white picket fence around the front yard. A gray minivan was in the driveway. The back bumper was filled with stickers for the town soccer league, "my student is an honor roll student at Lincoln Elementary School," and a stick family decal with a family of four, a dog and a cat. The front door opened, and a woman came out with two kids following behind her. *This is not Raymond's house. Must be the other one.*

Jay did what any police officer with a long night ahead of him would do. He hit the Dunkin Donuts drive thru, got a large sweetened iced tea and a glazed donut. Caffeine and sugar should help.

Jay sat outside the apartment building watching different people entering and exiting. By six o'clock, Jay was ready to stop for the day. He was hungry and needed to get home to Jake. Just then the front door of the building opened. A mother and her son came out followed by an older man. He appeared to be the same age as Dottie. Jay waited for him to turn around so he could see his face better. The man held the door for an elderly couple walking in and then stepped into the setting sun's light.

"Holy shit." Jay leaned forward in his seat. It was Emmaline's face staring back at him. But an older, male version of hers. "There he is." Jay couldn't believe it. He had found Em's dad. All the stories she had told him about her father. The man he had imagined in his head while listening to the memories Em had of all she and Dottie had been through. The man he imagined was extremely different than the man he was staring at now. Raymond Jacobs was a scrawny, older man of medium height. He had thin brown hair the same color as Emmaline's. Jay watched him walk down the sidewalk. *Even his walk is like Em's.* Jay was trying to imagine this tiny, frail man as a mentally ill abuser.

Jay started up his truck and slowly followed Raymond as he

walked down the street. As he got closer to him, he noticed the way the man's shoulders sagged forward. The way his head hung low like he was keeping his head down as if to avoid making eye contact with anyone. From what he could tell, life had been hard on this old man.

Jay stopped at the stop sign as Raymond Jacobs turned left at the corner. Jay wasn't sure if he should continue following him or drive away. Curiosity got the better of him and he followed Raymond. He pulled over at one point to let the car behind him pass. That was when he noticed Raymond was carrying something balled up in his hand. A string from the balled-up material had slipped out and was dangling next to the man's knee. It was an apron. Jay followed behind letting cars pass as needed. Finally, Raymond walked up the parking lot of the New Britain Diner. The place was closed, but as Raymond approached the building, he put his apron on, then walked to the back of the building. *What do you know, he works there?*

Jay was excited about all he had discovered. He had one question swirling around in his head. *Do I tell Emmaline?*

CHAPTER THIRTY-ONE

Emmaline

Emmaline was going stir crazy after being on bedrest for only three days. She still had twenty more weeks to go. She called her work to let them know what the doctor said. Maggie, her supervisor, told her not to worry. Her job was secure and would be there when she was ready to return. Maggie said her co-workers and the residents still wanted to throw her a baby shower if she was up to it. She said Josie would be handling all the arrangements. Emmaline was able to breathe easier knowing being out on bed rest would not hurt her employment. She loved working at the nursing home and knew she wanted to stay there if she could even after she got her registered nursing license.

Emmaline grabbed her laptop that was sitting next to her on the bed. She decided to do some research. Maybe while she had the time, she could begin studying for the state licensure exam to become a registered nurse. This had been her goal after she graduated with her associate's degree in nursing. After she got the job at The Village at River's Edge Nursing Home and started dating Jay, she kind of put it off. She had been enjoying her life and knew she would eventually take the exam. It was now three years later. Maybe being on bedrest was a blessing in disguise. She could focus on her pregnancy and study for the exam. Twenty weeks was a long time. She knew she could use the time to prepare for the baby and the next step in her career.

Emmaline heard conversation coming from down the hall. The front door squeaked itself closed. Every time they came over to her mom's house, Jay would say he was going to put some WD-40 on the hinges. She wouldn't allow it. She loved the sound of the old door. It was a cozy reminder of home. Jay appeared in the doorway of her bedroom. Emmaline wasn't expecting him. "Hey, what are you doing here?" She said it with a smile. He was handsome in his blue jeans and his black, mock turtleneck sweater. Emmaline realized she hadn't even showered yet.

"I thought we could have a movie date?" he smiled back at her. She noticed the crinkle lines at the corners of his eyes when he smiled. She hadn't seen his smile in a long time.

"You do know I'm supposed to be on bed rest. I don't know if a trip to the movies is included in that definition." She sat up a little straighter, brushing the hair out of her face.

"Well, I brought the movies to you." She hadn't noticed the shopping tote hanging by his side. He reached in and pulled out two sixteen-ounce bottles of soda. He walked over and handed one to her. Then a whiff of buttery goodness reached her nose.

"Is that what I think it is?" she asked.

"Sure is. I picked it up from AMC on the way over." He gingerly pulled out the bucket of popcorn from the bottom of the bag. "Extra salt, extra butter. Just the way you like it. What have you been up to today?"

Jay made his way to the other side of the bed. He handed her the popcorn and propped up the pillows next to her before sitting down spreading his long legs toward the end of the full-size bed. Once he was settled, Emmaline handed him back the bucket and put her laptop on her bedside table.

"I'm thinking about using this time on bedrest to study for my state license." She glanced over at him unsure of how he would react.

"That's incredible. A phenomenal idea. Can I do anything to help? Have you told Josie yet? I know she kept dropping hints about it last summer." Emmaline didn't realize he had picked up on Josie's hints. He never said anything to her about it. She would call Josie later and see if she wanted to study for them together.

Jay shifted in his spot, adjusting the pillows he had propped up behind his back. "I was actually thinking about swinging by the station, visiting with the crew and maybe talking to Bonetti about coming back to work on a part-time basis." She could see he was waiting for her response.

"Do you think you're ready of it?" she said as the worry began building in her stomach.

"I do. Since starting my rehab, I'm feeling better, stronger physically and mentally. I've been using the coping skills I've learned in therapy. I may struggle to recall things, but if I give myself time and use the association strategy I learned, I'm able to eventually get it or I ask for help. Yes, I am learning to ask for help." They laughed together. Jay had liked to be the helper, not the one who needed help. Emmaline had teased him about it many times. His big macho ego. "I wouldn't go back out on patrol. It's going to be a long time before I'm ready for the road. The occupational therapist I'm working with told me there were plenty of other things I can do that don't require me to expose myself to anything that would be a trigger for me. The more I thought about it, the more I knew he was right. I can do jobs at the station, fingerprinting, taking calls, community outreach, like at schools. I know I would like that."

"You might have to work up to it. Don't you think assemblies might be too overstimulating."

"Maybe, but classroom visits would be good. I know for myself, part of my rehab needs to include my job. Em, I miss it. I miss everyone, the camaraderie, serving the community. Even if it's a few half days a week to start, I need it."

"Then go talk to Bonetti. I'm sure everyone misses you and would love to have you back." Emmaline slid closer to Jay, resting her head on his shoulder, handing him the remote control to the TV. He placed his hand on her pregnant belly and scooped up a handful of popcorn with the other. A wave of contentment washed over him.

The day of her ultrasound had finally arrived. She hadn't discussed with Jay if they should find out the sex of the baby or not. Part of her wanted to know and another part wanted to wait. Jay picked her up at two p.m. They drove over to her doctor's office in West Hartford. The sun was at its peak as they went over the mountain into the city. The sun was warm on her face. She closed her eyes and took in the heat of the sun's rays on her face enjoying some extra vitamin D. Now that spring was finally here, she needed to get outside more. She missed running and being outdoors.

Jay doted on her like she was a fragile, porcelain doll. He helped her in and out of the car. He held her hand walking her from the car to the building entrance. They waited quietly together in the exam room while the nurse went through all of her protocol. Finally, Dr. Sahakyan came into the room. "How are the soon-to-be-parents doing today?"

"Excited, "Jay said.

"Nervous," Emmaline said simultaneously.

Dr. Sahakyan laughed at the two of them. Emmaline was sure she had probably seen couples like them a million times before.

"How is bed rest going for you?" she asked as she put jelly on the ultrasound wand.

"I'm doing okay. The bleeding has gotten much better. A little spotting here and there. Nothing bad. I decided to use the time to study for my state nursing certification." Emmaline tried not to squirm when the cold of the jelly hit her stomach.

"Good for you. And work?"

"They have been supportive." The doctor adjusted a knob on the machine and the whooshing sound of their baby's heartbeat echoed in the room. Emmaline turned to Jay. His smile was as big as hers. He held her hand as they watched the image of their child come onto the screen in its black and white form. They could see the side profile of the head, the little eye, nose, and mouth. The baby's arms and legs were moving around. "Oh," The baby gave a kick and Emmaline felt it right below her belly button.

"Look who decided to say hi." Dr. Sahakyan moved the wand around. They watched the baby swimming around in her womb. "The placenta still hasn't moved. Our goal is to get you to thirty-four weeks. After that we can schedule a c-section. Only thirteen more weeks to go. It may sound like a lot but believe me when I tell you it will go fast. I would like to see you every two weeks until then so we can monitor you both. Did you want to know the sex of your baby?" The doctor looked from Emmaline to Jay and back to Emmaline.

"No," they both said it at the same time. They hadn't even discussed it, yet they were both on the same page. They wanted to wait.

Jay held Emmaline's hand as they drove away from the hospital. She glanced over at him. She couldn't quite make out the expression on his face.

"Do you mind if we stop somewhere before I take you back to your mom's?"

"I guess," she wasn't sure where he wanted to go but she was fine not going back to her bed for a little bit longer. It felt good to be out for a change.

Jay drove them over to River Glen Little League field in Farmington. Emmaline had been here a few times to watch Jay play baseball in the adult league. She stared at the fields as they drove in. There were teams in uniform on the diamond and in the outfield. "A little league game?"

"It may not be the Red Sox, but I thought maybe we could watch a baseball game together. The concession stand might even be open. Are you up for a hot dog and chips with disgusting nacho cheese?"

Emmaline was touched by his thoughtfulness. She was not sure if the old Jay would have done the same. "The grosser the better. Sounds perfect."

Jay parked the car in the closest spot to the bleachers. He helped her walk over to the first row. "Be right back," he said and headed over to the concession stand. He came back a few minutes later with a concession box stuffed with two hot dogs, nachos, cheese and two drinks. They sat in silence eating and watching the game. The boys who were playing were around middle school age. Emmaline thought about Jay and Scottie at this age playing together.

"Do you miss it?" she asked.

"What? Playing baseball. Yeah. Maybe next summer I'll be able to play again. I'll have to wait and see. Who knows? Maybe I'll end up coaching instead if our little nugget decides they want to play." He bumped her shoulder with his in a joking fashion.

They finished up their early dinner while watching the game. Jay threw away the garbage and sat back down next to her. "Do you ever think about your dad?" The question took her by surprise. She wasn't expecting it.

"Sometimes. I wonder where he is. If he's doing better. Sometimes I wonder if I could let go of who he was in my mind if I knew he was better now. Like if mom kicking him out was what he needed to finally get help."

"Have you ever thought of looking for him?" Jay asked as the batter hit a line drive to left field. They both cheered with the other fans on the bleachers.

"I wouldn't even know where to begin to find him."

"There is this thing called Google you know. You can find almost anyone on it." He knocked her knee with his teasing her. *This is nice*, Em thought to herself.

Emmaline was tired by the time they got back to Dottie's house. It wasn't much of a day on bed rest, but she felt good. She filled her mom in on her doctor's appointment, thanked Jay for spending the day with her and then headed down the hallway to her room. She was asleep before her head hit the pillow. She awoke a bit later to the sound of whispered arguing coming from down the hall. Emmaline slowly sat up so she could tune into the voices. She heard her mom, Jay, and Viv. She couldn't imagine what they could be arguing about. Maybe Jay was trying to convince her mom it would be best for her to be home at the cabin.

As she walked down the hallway the whispered voices grew louder. They were coming from the kitchen. She knew her mom and Viv were in there baking. Was Jay in there helping them, she wondered. Suddenly she heard her mom's voice. "I did it to protect her. I figured when she was ready, she would ask."

Protect her, from what? Emmaline was in the living room eavesdropping from outside the doorway to the kitchen.

"If you ask me, she should never know the whereabouts of that jackass. I don't care how good he is doing." Viv's voice reverberated through her ears.

Are they talking about my father? She leaned in closer so as not to miss anything.

"Viv, stop. You know I don't like keeping secrets from her. She went through so much as a child because of him. I figured when she got older and brought it up, I'd tell her."

"Don't you think she has a right to know?" Jay asked.

"If she wants to know."

"Well, I don't want to keep secrets from my wife. We've been through enough these past months. I'd like to give her the option of seeing him again if she wants to. Maybe it will bring her some closure. Maybe if she were able to see him, talk to him, she would stop comparing me to him. I don't want our marriage to be ruined over things he did."

Emmaline walked into the kitchen. The three of them turned and stared at her. No words were spoken. They were all staring at her like they were waiting to see if she had heard them. "You know where Dad is?"

Dottie took a deep breath and sighed heavily before answering, "Yes."

"When did you find out?"

"Since the day I threw him out. I've known where he was and how he was doing."

"All this time, you knew." Emmaline looked at her mother confused. "I lived in fear for years he might walk through the door. Always afraid, he'd have an episode, go into a rage, and come after us."

"Em, I did it for that reason. To protect you. To make sure he couldn't just show up. Jim didn't share all the details about your father because he couldn't. But I needed to know we were safe, and I wanted to make sure he was okay. I felt a sense of responsibility for your father." Dottie walked over to Emmaline, but she held a hand up to stop her mother. Em couldn't take in all of the information coming at her.

"Dr. Jim knows. Knows where Dad is? How is he doing?" She was so confused. How did all these people in her life know about her own father, but her?

"Jim was one of your father's doctors. His team has been helping your dad since he moved out. I'm sorry, honey. I didn't tell you to keep it a secret from you. I thought I was protecting you. I thought as long as I knew where he was and how he was doing we were safe. You were finally living a stable life, and I didn't want your father's illness to upset our stability. I hope you're not angry with me."

Emmaline walked over to the kitchen table and sat down in a chair. "I'm not angry. I don't know how to feel. I need some time to process this." Viv and her mom started talking at once about the past, her father, the circumstances, the treatment, and medication he was getting. Vivian cursed him out, while Dottie explained her choices over the past fourteen years of Em's life without him.

Emmaline glanced over at Jay who was standing off to the side leaning against the counter. "Can I come back to the cabin with you?"

Jay stood up. "Of course."

"Em, wait don't go. Please, let's talk about this." Dottie's voice choked up.

Emmaline stood up, walked over to her mother, and gave her a hug. "Mom, I'm not mad. I need time to think. I love you and everything you've done for me. You have kept me safe. You gave me a happy life after dad was gone. I can't imagine how hard what you did for me must have been. I appreciate you. I want to go home. I want to sleep in my bed. I want to think. Okay?"

"Good girl," Viv added her two cents in. "You do what's best for you. I've got your mom."

"What so you can try to hit me over the head again with a rolling pin?" They all let out an uncomfortable laugh.

"Hey, I apologized already for that. My medication was screwing with my head. I should have taken a rolling pin to you years ago when Raymond started to go all loco. Saved you both from years of suffering." Viv walked over to her niece and wrapped her in a hug. "Listen to me girlie. You want to be one of us sassy old broads, you keep doing what's best for you and screw the rest. Now take this handsome husband home, your dog's probably pissed all over the floors by now."

Jake and Emmaline eyes met; they had completely forgotten about Jake.

CHAPTER THIRTY-TWO

Emmaline

On the way to the cabin, Emmaline's mind was racing thinking about her father. Memories of him flashed through her mind. She wondered what he looked like now. She wondered if she would recognize him or if he would recognize her.

"I want to see my dad," she said with conviction.

"Are you sure?"

Emmaline could hear the concern in Jay's voice.

"Yes. I don't know if I'm ready to talk to him, but I want to see him. I want to see what he looks like now. I need to, Jay. There is an urgency pulling at me to see him."

"Okay. I can take you to see him."

"Wait, you know where he is?" Emmaline turned to Jay. She was taken aback. "How? Did Jim tell you?"

"You know I am a police officer." He smirked at her. Then he filled her in on how he tracked her father down. "Let's swing by the cabin first. We can let Jake out and take him with us for a ride."

"Can we text Scottie and ask him to swing by the house?" Emmaline thought about it for a moment. "Actually, I take that back. I think I would like Jake with us. An extra layer of protection with having our big, black labrador who barks at strangers by my side."

Jake was excited when they arrived at the cabin. Emmaline had missed her boy. They had trained him not to jump on people, but she wished he could jump into her arms. "Hey boy, want to go for a ride in the car?" His silky, black ears perked up at the word car. He flew into the open door Jay held for him and took his spot in the backseat of the truck's cabin sticking his head between Jay and Emmaline's seats. Jake was panting and smiling his doggy smile at the same time.

"Where is he now?" Emmaline asked.

"He lives in an apartment in New Britain and works down the road around the corner at a local diner. I don't know if it's his only job or not. Going by his schedule from the other day, he should be at work at this time. We can drive over to the diner first. If we don't see any signs of him, we can go to the apartment."

"Okay, sounds good." Emmaline couldn't put a finger on all of the emotions flowing between her heart, head, and stomach. She was nervous, excited, scared, curious. As if Jay could sense her racing thoughts he reached over and grabbed her hand.

"You doing okay?" he said.

"Yes, no, I don't know. I don't know what I expect. I know I don't want to talk to him, and I know I need to see him. I have to see him. I want to see if he still has the crazed look in his eyes like when he would go into a full-blown rage. If he's getting treatment, is he different or the same? When I imagine him in my mind's eyes, I see the face of my father from the last time we were all together. He was manic with joy and fun; we were all laughing at his silliness and then in a flash his laughter became rage as he thought we were making fun of him. 'I'll show you how funny I can be' he said and then came after us. The blows came so fast. We weren't prepared. Mom dove at me to intersect a couple of his swings. She screamed at me to go to my room and lock the door. He tried to chase after me, but she grabbed his leg and pulled. He went down hard and hit his chin on the corner of the kitchen table. The last eye contact we made was with me at the kitchen doorway and his impact with the table. Our eyes met and I saw what I can only describe as a creature-like stare which turned to utter sadness in his eyes as his body hit the floor. What I would think of when a werewolf has been causing havoc all night and then the sun comes up and he becomes human again and realizes what he's done."

"I can't believe you used that analogy. I was telling Heather, my therapist, how I feel like I switch between Bruce Banner and The Hulk. Since starting therapy and learning how to control the anger and frustration things have been much better. Who knows, maybe Jim's team has done the same for your dad." Jay squeezed her hand, sending an electric current of hope and warmth to her heart. It occurred to her how easily they had fallen back into step over the last week. It was the same as before and yet different, gentler. She liked it.

Jay pulled into an old fifty's style diner. It was closed. The paint on the sign had weathered off. She could see the top of leather booths through the windows. It definitely could use a face lift, but it was still so inviting. A classic, old diner. "Here we are." Jay backed the truck into the furthest spot so they could park, looking into the windows without making it too obvious they were casing the joint.

"What does he do here?" She pulled her sunglasses off to get a clearer view through the large windows.

"I'm not sure. The day I was here he walked in with an apron. Maybe a cook or busboy."

"Cook? I could see him being a cook. He was always whipping up fun stuff in the kitchen. Chicken and waffles were his specialty." They sat in silence watching for any movement in the diner. Jake looked between them as if to ask if they were going to get out of the car or not. Emmaline pet his head as she continued to watch. Suddenly, a thin, scraggly man wearing a white apron walked around from the back of the diner. He was carrying two bags of trash. Emmaline watched him walk the bags to the dumpster at the far corner of the parking lot. When he turned around, she saw it. Her own face staring back at her. "Holy shit, Jay. It's him."

Emmaline reached over and grabbed Jay's bicep tightly. She looked from her father to Jay in complete shock. "It's him." Her eyes began to water, her heart raced. She watched her father, Raymond Jacobs, take a pack of cigarettes out of his shirt pocket and a lighter from his jeans. He shook the pack of cigarettes until one popped out. He lit the cigarette and put his lighter back. It was as if the world was moving in slow motion. Emmaline watched him inhale from the cigarette and exhale the smoke. It didn't seem to faze her father how there was a random black truck in the parking lot.

"Do you want to go talk to him?" Emmaline jerked her head over to Jay.

"What? No. No, I'm not ready. I just wanted to see him. He looks the same. Older, thinner, but not scary. He looks kind of... sad."

"That's what I thought too when I realized it was him. He has a sadness about him. As if he is carrying around the weight of regrets on his shoulders and can't stand up straight anymore."

"Exactly. As he should. Maybe. I don't know. I can't describe the emotions I'm having right now except I think I can finally let go of the image I have of him in mind. I don't have to be afraid that he is going to come back for us. Even if he tried. I think I could blow him over with one breath. He's so thin now." They watched Raymond finish his cigarette, drop it on the ground and put it out with the toe of his black sneaker. He then leaned over and picked the butt off the ground and walked away. "He's litter conscious. That's nice."

"Are you ready to go home?"

"Yes, can we drive by his apartment building. I'd like to see it."

"Of course." Jay started the truck and drove the few streets over to the apartment building he first saw Raymond walk out of. Emmaline stayed quiet as she they drove slowly by the place where her father was living. She remained quiet on the ride back to the cabin.

Once back at their home, Emmaline walked right up the stairs to their bedroom as if it was any other day. She was emotionally and physically drained from the day. She texted her mom quickly to reassure her all was fine, and she would be sleeping at the cabin. She didn't bother to wash her face or brush her teeth. She crawled into her side of the bed and went to sleep.

Emmaline woke up disoriented. She caught a glimpse of the sun shining through the blinds. Slowly sitting up, she glanced around the room remembering she was at the cabin and not her mom's house. *I saw my dad last night.* The thought popped into her head. "Holy shit, I saw my dad last night." She glanced around the room again and then over to Jay's side of the bed. It hadn't been disturbed. It was still made up from the day before. Emmaline wondered if Jay slept in the guest bedroom. She slowly got out of bed. It was getting hard to get off things as her belly grew bigger.

She walked down the stairs being extra careful as she descended. Emmaline heard an unfamiliar noise. When she reached the bottom few steps, she saw Jay riding a bike on a trainer by the fireplace. He hadn't noticed her yet as he had his AirPods in his ears. The house seemed lighter to Em. Vastly different from the darkness that had clouded over it when she left on Christmas Eve. He finally noticed her.

"Hey, how did you sleep?" he asked pulling one of his ear buds out of his ear.

"Good. Really good actually. Where did you sleep?"

"I fell asleep on the couch watching baseball with Jake. By the time I woke up, it was the middle of the night. I didn't want to disturb you, so I rolled over and went back to sleep." He smiled his big, beautiful smile that lit up his whole face while he continued to pedal.

"That thing is pretty neat." She walked over to him and the bike.

"Yeah, this is what the crew chipped in and got me. I've only taken it out on the road that one time. It was a little bit of a hairy experience. I think when I do go back out it will be on the bike trail to start. I'm still a little wary with cars and intersections."

She nodded. "Can I give it a try?"

"Sure." Jay slowed down his pace and then hopped off to help her on. "Wait, is it okay for you to be doing this?"

"I'll be careful. I want to try it. It's been ages since I've been on a bike. I miss running. I can't stand being still all the time. Especially since I'm not working. I know it's what's best for the baby and me but sitting around all day gets super boring."

"Now you know how I've felt." Emmaline met his eyes. He was right, she hadn't understood what it must be like for him to not be able to do all the things he was able to do before the accident. She was so fixated on him returning to his old self she wasn't thinking much about his present self. "I'm sorry if I have been hard on you since the accident."

Jay looked at her shocked. "Em, you weren't hard on me. I wouldn't listen. Everyone was giving me all the support I needed to get better; I was the one being hard on myself. I thought I could do it all on my own. I'm learning in therapy my traumatic brain injury is beyond my control. Now, I'm learning to control what I can and use my tools to help me cope with what I can't.

I'm accepting my limitations. I resisted treatment I could have had from the start. I'm sorry to you. I put us both through more than we needed to and risked our relationship because of my ego."

Emmaline sat on the bike after Jay adjusted the seat for her. "You don't need to apologize to me. Actually, no more apologies. I hoped for so long you would reach a point where you made the decision on your own, and you did." She started pedaling slowly and then increased the speed. "Wow, this is fun. Maybe after the baby is born, I can get a bike with one of those baby seats and we can all hit the trail together."

"That would be amazing. I'd love for us to be able to take family bike rides." She saw Jay glance over at the clock. "I have to jump in the shower. I have my therapy appointment soon. You could come with me if you want to?" Jay watched her with his brown, puppy dog eyes waiting for her answer.

"I would like to." She smiled at him and slowly got off the bike. "I'll go get ready."

"I'll carry you up the stairs." Jay walked toward her taking her hand and supporting her by placing a hand on her low back.

"You don't need to carry me up, but walking behind me would be great. Thank you."

Once they were both ready, they got in the truck and headed back to New Britain and the Hospital for Special Care. Jay had to help hoist Emmaline into the passenger seat. "Between your truck and my Jeep, I think we may need to consider a better car for the baby. In the meantime, I may have to swap cars with Mom."

Emmaline felt like she should be nervous going to Jay's doctor appointment with him, meeting his team of therapists. But she wasn't. Spending these past couple of weeks with Jay has shown her how much it is helping him. Jay gave her the walking tour as they made their way down different hallways to Heather's office.

"Hey Jay, come on in. Oh, hi. You must be Emmaline. How cute you are with your baby bump. How are you feeling? I hope you don't mind Jay has filled me in on what's been going on." Heather had a welcoming demeanor. Emmaline felt comfortable with her immediately. Heather seemed only a few years older than she and Jay. She seemed like someone she would go out to coffee with or grab drinks with after work. Em could tell she was the type of person who was easy to talk to.

"Of course not. You are his therapist. I assumed he would talk to you. I hoped he would talk to you." They all chuckled as everyone sat down. "Thanks for allowing me to join you both."

"Of course. It's all part of the recovery process. TBI's effect the caretakers as much as they affect the patients. You would be amazed at how many families I have counseled in addition to the TBI patients. Depending on the severity of the injury, it can change your whole life. Now tell me what's been going on since I last saw you, Jay."

Emmaline listened as Jay talked about the events of the last week. It was interesting to hear him be so open and forthcoming in detail about everything including how it all affected him. He had never been good at expressing his emotions unless it was the two of them alone together. He finally got to the part about her dad and them visiting his work so Emmaline could see him from a distance.

"Emmaline, what was it like for you to see your father after all of this time." Heather turned her attention over to her.

"Strange, very strange."

"Tell me more."

"He's old, thin. Not as intimidating as the man I remember.

What were we saying, Jay? Oh, I remember. He looked sad. Like he's carrying a lot of burden on his shoulders."

"He probably is. Regret can add a lot on to a body mentally and physically. Now that you have seen him, do you have any interest in speaking with him? Do you want to have any kind of relationship with him?" Em realized the therapy session had switched from Jay's session to hers.

"I don't know if I want a relationship with him. Now that I have seen him, I do think I want to talk to him. The little girl in me wants to confront him, yell at him about all the damage he did to me and my mom. The adult woman knows he was ill, and his disease was not being treated. If I talked to him then maybe it would resolve the issues I've still been carrying from my childhood." Emmaline glanced down at her hands. She felt a little ashamed to admit it out loud.

"What will it resolve for you?" Heather asked tenderly.

"That he no longer has power over me." Emmaline whispered not meeting either of their eyes.

"Have you felt like he has had that even after all these years? Power over you?" Heather questioned her. Jay sat by her side quietly giving her this time with Heather.

"I think there was a fear inside, because we," she corrected herself, "I...didn't know where he was. There was a piece of me afraid he would have an episode and come find us. That he would come back in a rage. He would really hurt us or kill us." Jay reached over and grabbed her trembling hands and held them in his.

"Jay, would you mind if I talked to Emmaline for a few minutes, just the two of us."

"Of course not." Jay stood up, kissed Emmaline on the top of her head. He walked out of the office, closing the door behind him.

"Does Jay remind you of your dad?" Heather asked.

"No, at least old Jay never did. He was always smiling, laughing, life of the party, but cared for everyone. Since the accident, this new Jay is different."

"How so?" Heather leaned forward on her desk, meeting her eyes with Emmaline's.

"He's more emotional, cries easy." She laughed a little. "He gets upset easily. He's moody. He gets frustrated with himself and with me. But also, he's quieter, gentler in a way. Old Jay was loving but this is different. More like doting. This Jay doesn't have to be going all the time. Old Jay always had one foot out the door ready for the next thing to happen. He was fun, exciting, and adventurous. We did everything. We ran together, went to baseball games, trivia nights, BBQs with friends, outings with the crew at the station or my work. I tried to do a couple of those things with him after the accident. I tried to get back to our normal life and it was a disaster. He would get frustrated with himself, angry at me. He would snap over the littlest things. He was agitated all the time. It made it hard to be around him. Nothing I did ever seemed to make him happy."

"He's not there yet, but that doesn't mean he won't be, to some degree, at some point. You'll need to modify the activities, but it doesn't mean he won't enjoy them again one day. Right now, his brain and body won't let him. They still need time to heal. To learn how to process information and feelings despite his brain injury. And that is okay?"

"Of course it is. I'm the one who has always been more of the homebody. It was old Jay who had to have plans. We had to be doing something all the time. I loved it at the time, but now it's nice not having to constantly be doing something, planning something. Not that I can in my condition anyway." She exaggerated by rubbing her belly, smiling down at her bump.

"You keep saying old Jay and new Jay. Why not just Jay?"

Heather asked her without judgment in her tone. Emmaline flushed with embarrassment.

"You sound like my best friend Josie. She tells me I need to stop comparing the two. She says he's the same Jay at the core."

Heather adjusted herself back in her chair. "Smart girl. Let's go back to your dad. If you confronted your father, what would you say to him?"

"I'm not sure. Since seeing him from a distance, knowing where he is, where he works and lives. It's like my inner child is tugging at my hand telling me to go talk to him."

"Would it help you to move forward in your marriage. Would it help you to let go of your concerns that Jay will be the same father you had to your child."

"I don't know. Maybe." Heather stood up, walked around her desk, and called Jay back in through the crack of her open door. Jay came back in and sat down in the spot next to Emmaline. He looked at her with curiosity waiting to be filled in on what she had talked about with Heather.

Heather sat in the extra chair next to her desk meeting them both at eye level. "It's only been seven months since the accident and in a short amount of time you've both been through a lot. We all have moments in our lives when something happens, and we have to decide from this day forward how will I move on. You got married. You made beautiful plans for building a life together and then the accident happened. A shift happened and it will happen many more times in your life. What you both have to decide is from this day forward, like the vows you took on your wedding day, for better or worse, how you will move forward from this moment. I promise you this will not be the last time in your marriage you will have to make tough decisions together. You now have to decide how you will handle these situations when they happen, as a united team or at opposite sides of the court. I have homework for you. I'm going to write it down and give it to Jay." Heather reached across her desk and pulled a pad and a pen to a closer spot near here. She wrote down something on the piece of paper, folded it up and grabbed an envelope from her desk caddy. Emmaline watched her put the paper in the envelope and use the self-sealing strip to close it up. "When you think you're ready to answer that question open this envelope. That's your homework."

Heather handed the envelope to Jay who put it in his back pocket.

On the drive back home, Emmaline told Jay she wanted to talk to her father. She needed to confront him to be able to put all of the images which have been flashing in her mind of her childhood out of her head. She wanted to put the past in the past and leave it there.

"What will you say to him?"

"I have no idea." Emmaline turned her head to gaze out the passenger side window. Her mind drifted off to the man she saw smoking a cigarette behind the diner the day before. She couldn't believe she saw her father. The same man who could make her laugh until she wet her pants or would terrify her to the point that she would hide under her bed from his rage.

CHAPTER THIRTY-THREE

Jay

After they got back to the cabin, Jay helped Emmaline upstairs to rest. She wanted time to herself to think and nap. Jay was restless. As much as Emmaline felt that pull to see her father, Jay had the same urgency coursing through himself to go to the station. He texted Emmaline to let her know his plan. She texted him back wishing him good luck with Lieutenant Bonetti.

It took Jay about twenty-five minutes to drive over to the station in Farmington. He spent the drive over going through everything he wanted to say to Bonetti to convince him to let him come back on a part-time basis. Once there he sat in his parked truck for a few minutes staring at the entrance. He hadn't been through the station doors since he was put on medical leave. *Now or never.* He said to himself as he got out of the truck and clicked the lock button on his key fob.

Part of him wanted to sneak in a back door to get to Bonetti's office. The other part of him wanted to walk through the front door like he used to saying hello to everyone on his way through the station. He decided to go for it. This was his crew; these people were his family. He grabbed the handle to the door, took a breath and walked in.

The first thing Jay noticed was the smell. It smelled like the station; a mixture of coffee, floor cleaner, and poly-cotton blend. A combination he loved. As Jay walked through the station, his colleagues came over to him saying hello, asking him how he was doing, congratulating him on the baby. He thanked them all for the bike and trainer. They filled him in on all the happenings around the station while he'd been gone. It was like he had only been gone over a weekend. It felt so good to be back with his crew. He saw Lieutenant Bonetti off in the distance. Bonetti walked over to where he was standing.

"Well, well...look who came to visit." Bonetti said, putting his hand out toward him.

"Good to see you, Lieutenant." Jay shook the senior officer's hand.

"How are you? How's Emmaline doing?" The people around them slowly dispersed leaving Jay and Bonetti to talk by themselves.

"She's good. We're good. Actually, if you have a few minutes, I was hoping I could talk to you."

"Sure, let's go into my office." Bonetti walked in front of Jay who followed him back to his office. Once inside, the lieutenant closed the door to give them some privacy. "What's going on? How's your rehab going?"

Jay filled him in on his treatment plan, the progress he had been making. He was also honest with him about his migraines and how easily he can be overstimulated by lights, sounds or too much stimuli at once which can lead to agitation, outbursts, and migraines. "Sir, I'd like to come back on limited work hours if possible. I'm still working on myself, and I think coming back to work would help with my rehab." Jay leaned forward in his chair putting his elbows on his knees. "Sir, I need this. It gives me purpose. Being a police officer is part of my identity, and I need my identity back. I know I can't be in a patrol car yet. But there must be some things here at the station that I can do."

Bonetti sat back in his chair rocking slowly back and forth, silently for a few moments. He tented his fingers together, resting them on his belly while staring at Jay. Jay stared back in anticipation. Worry washed over him that Bonetti was going to turn him down. "Okay."

"Okay? Really." Jay jumped up out of his chair. It was not the answer he was expecting. "I promise I'll do everything I can and anything that is too much I'll be honest and let you know."

"When were you thinking of returning?" Bonetti asked still in the same position.

"I was hoping within the next couple of weeks?"

"Don't you have a baby on the way? Maybe we should wait until after the baby comes and you are all home and settled in."

"I did think of that. I spoke with my therapist about it too. We agreed it would be good for me to start back to work slowly. I can get used to being back at work. Then the baby will come, and I'll adapt to that change as well. I'm excited. It's the first time in a long time I've been excited for the future ahead."

Lieutenant Bonetti stood up from his chair and walked around his desk. "I'm happy for you, Jay. I'm really happy for you. We have missed you around here. I'm going to talk to the captain, I'll talk to HR, and we'll make arrangements for you to come back on a limited basis to start."

"Thank you, sir. I can't tell you how much I appreciate this." Jay shook the lieutenant's hand. As he headed out of the office door, he looked around the station at all the faces. He felt lighter in his heart at the thought of coming back. He couldn't wait to put his uniform back on.

Jay walked out the door of the station with a grin on his face. He headed toward the parking lot and the rows of cars. His mind was drawing a blank. *What do I drive? I drive a...I drive a...*complete blank. He saw sedans, minivans, SUVs, and trucks. Nothing was clicking for him.

"Hey Jay," a loud voice from behind called out as a hand slapped him on the shoulder. "Forget where you parked your truck. It happens to me all the time. Yours is hard to miss though. That bright black beauty over there is an eye catcher."

Jay turned to where the man was pointing and then glanced back to the man. *I know him. A, B, C, D, E, F..F. Fred, Frank. Yes, Frank.*

"Thanks, Frank. I think I may need to put a tracking device on it." They both laughed.

"We've missed you around here. Hope to see you back soon," Frank said heading to his own car.

"You will. A couple more weeks and I'll be back. See you then," Jay waved back at the man as he walked toward his truck.

Once inside his truck, Jay took a moment to process what had happened. He was returning to work. He couldn't remember Frank's name and he used another skill. The skill he learned in treatment to remember something worked. As Dr. Jim would say, it is another tool for his toolbox. He was taking more steps to recovery and felt good about it.

Before leaving the station, Jay pulled his cell phone out of his pocket. He wanted to check on Emmaline and see if she needed anything before he went home. He saw a missed text from her.

> **Emmaline:** I want to talk to my dad. Can you make it happen? Can you text Jim for me?

> **Jay:** You got it. See you soon.

Jay pulled up Dr. Jim's contact information in his cell phone. He hit the message icon in his contacts app.

> **Jay:** Emmaline wants to meet with her dad. Can you set it up?

Jay sent the message and put his phone back in his front pocket. Jay waited a few minutes for an answer while warming up his truck. He thought about Emmaline back at the cabin. How natural it felt having her home. *Please stay.* He thought to himself. He never wanted his wife to leave again. He would do anything to make sure that didn't happen. He hoped talking to her father would bring her peace. All he wanted was for her to know she was safe with him again. He wanted her to trust him. He needed her to believe he would never do anything to harm her or their baby. He had filled his prescription and started taking the medication daily. His migraines and their severity had gone down. He even felt his daily anxiety subsided. He was working in therapy to deal with a variety of situations if they arise. He was stronger in his body mentally and physically.

Jay felt the phone in his pocket buzz with an incoming text message. He pulled the phone back out of his pocket. It was a text back from Jim. Jay opened his phone and read the text.

> **Dr. Jim:** Hey Jay, I spoke with Raymond. How about Saturday at the diner? It's a safe space for him. Would eleven in the morning work for her?

> **Jay:** I'll ask Em, but let's plan on it unless you hear different from me.

Jay felt nervous for Emmaline. He had felt the conviction in her to settle things with her. He hoped seeing her father would bring her what she needed. Regardless of how it went, he would be by her side. He started his truck and threw the gear shift into drive. Time to go home to his wife.

CHAPTER THIRTY-FOUR

Emmaline

Emmaline had peed what felt like twenty times already that morning. She didn't know if it was the baby sitting on her bladder or because of the nerves coursing through her body. She was seeing her father today. The first time in fourteen years. She was terrified. Jay had made a comment about her pacing through the house. She couldn't stop. It was what she did when she was worried about something.

"Do you know what you are going to say to him?" Jay's gaze followed her back and forth across the living room floor.

"I don't know. Believe me, I've had many conversations with him in my head, but none of them were the start of the conversation. Usually, it was me screaming at him for being a complete asshole and a shit father. I want to tell him he ruined men for me. I had trust issues for years until I met you." She pointed toward Jay as she passed him while pacing. Jay was sitting on the arm of the couch watching her. "I also want to tell him I know he was sick. I'm sorry he was suffering, and nobody knew enough to help him. I want to know if he is better now. That leaving was the best thing for him. I want him to know mom and I are great. We did fine without him. I want to say I'm glad I got to talk to him, and I never want to see him again."

"It sounds like you know exactly what you want to say." Jay stood up, walked over to her, and stopped her in mid-pace. He pulled her into a hug. "I will be wherever you want me to be, next to you or in the truck. Whatever you need."

Emmaline rested her head in her spot on his shoulder. The place she fit perfectly. The one that had first told her she was home. "Okay, let's do this." She squeezed him tighter for extra reassurance.

～

Emmaline sat in the truck staring at the front entrance to the diner. They had arrived fifteen minutes early. She was second guessing her decision with all of the extra time waiting for their meeting. "I'm doing the right thing, right?" She asked nervously.

"Yes."

"This will be good for me," she said more to herself then to him.

"Yes."

"Yeah, that's what I think too." Emmaline saw Dr. Jim walking through the parking lot. She sat up a little straighter as she watched him walk through the diner's entrance. *He's inside. He's going to meet up with dad.* "I'm going in." Emmaline started to unbuckle her seat belt. Jay reached over placing his hand on hers.

"Are you sure you don't want me to come in with you?" He met her eyes.

"No. I need to do this myself. Jim's there. That will help." She finished unbuckling her seatbelt and opened the door. She heard Jay jump out of his side of the truck and watched him come around to her side to help her out. "Thank you."

He pulled her into a supportive hug, whispering into her ear,

"I'm here if you need me." She nodded in agreement and slowly made her way to the front door, her belly leading the way.

Emmaline walked through the front entrance and scanned the diner for a familiar face. Dr. Jim was a tall man which made it easier for Em to spot the booth he was in with her father. She made eye contact with Jim. She wasn't ready to match eyes with her father yet. Jim got up from the table and walked over to her. "Are you ready?"

"I think so." Emmaline let go of the breath she had been holding in.

"He's been wanting to see you for a long time. I'll be right here the whole time." Jim put his hand on her back and helped guide her across the floor. Emmaline was thankful for his support as she couldn't seem to get her feet to move on their own. As they approached the table, Emmaline finally met eyes with her father. He seemed much older up close. He had the wrinkles in his face of a man who had been smoking most of his life. Below his eyes were large, dark bags. He looked like a weathered fisherman. He slowly rose from the table. He stood a few inches taller than her. She watched him look her over. She saw him notice her pregnant belly. Then he stared directly into her eyes.

"Hi, Emmaline," he said and then put his head down.

"Hi Dad." Emmaline sat down in the booth across from where he was sitting. She glanced up at Jim to see which side of the table he would sit on.

"I will let you two get reacquainted. I'll be sitting at a stool at the counter if you need anything." Emmaline's anxiety was building up inside. She wanted to telepathically say to Jim, *please, don't leave us.* "Give a holler if you need me," he said reassuringly to both of them. Emmaline glanced over at her father. He had the same look in his eyes as she did. It hadn't even occurred to her that he might be as nervous about their meeting as she was. They watched Jim walk away and then turned to each other. They sat for a few beats in an awkward silence.

"Congratulations on your baby," her father finally said.

"Thank you."

"When are you due?"

"The end of May."

"So, I guess that means I'm going to be a grandpa," he said with a half-smile at her.

Emmaline put her head down for a moment. She was twisting her hands around in her lap. She didn't say anything in response. She didn't know what to say. The father she remembered from her childhood she would never let near her own child. This man across from her was a complete stranger in a weird, familiar way. "Thanks for meeting with me today," she said instead.

"I've been wanting to see you, talk to you. I made your mom a promise. After everything I put you both through, I figured keeping my promise to Dottie was the least I could do. You're so grown up." He fidgeted with the coffee mug in front of him.

A waitress came over to take their order. Emmaline asked for a cup of tea, nothing to eat. Her father told the waitress he would only be having coffee. After she left, Emmaline gathered the courage to finally speak honestly with him.

"I lived in fear for so long that you would return to hurt mom and me. I jumped at every creak I heard in the house; I glanced over my shoulder constantly worried you might be following me; I had nightmares for years. Mom would reassure me you weren't coming back. I didn't believe her. At the same time, there was a part of me which held out hope you would come back and be okay. You'd be the loving father I got glimpses of occasionally. Part of me knew that man was in there, but the demon side of you dominated in the end." Emmaline picked up her cup of tea and blew on it before taking a sip.

"Em, I can never apologize enough for the person I was. For

all I put you and your mom through. I was sick. I didn't want to see it. My dad was the same way. I thought of it as normal dad behavior, that's how sick I was I couldn't even recognize how wrong my outbursts were. Your mom kicking me out was best for everyone. You didn't have to be subjected to my mental illness and abuse anymore. It wasn't fair to you to have to be afraid in your own home. If it wasn't for your mom contacting Jim and him finding me, I would probably be dead by now. I was a victim of my own mind. I need you to know I take my medication consistently, I go to group therapy, I live a quiet life, I am not a threat to you anymore. I won't hurt you or your family." As she listened to her father the anger in her started to dissolve. She came in wanting to yell and scream at this man who had hurt her and her mom for so long. This man who had destroyed her early years with his manic behavior. This man who made her afraid to be cared for by anyone for a long time. Her anger was melting down into a pool of pity.

"I came here ready to tell you what a shit of a father you were. I wanted to yell at you for ruining my childhood. To scream at you for all the mental and physical scars you left on me. For hurting mom. For ruining men for me. But I'm not the same little girl you once knew. Mom did a fantastic job of raising me and giving me the happiest childhood she could. She and Aunt Viv gave me unconditional love. My husband showed me trust and safety in a man's arms. I know you were sick. I'm sorry you were suffering and lost your family because of it. I'm sorry we couldn't help you."

"Em, I—" He started to say something, but she held her hand up.

"Please let me finish. I need to get this out." He nodded. "I'm glad you're doing better now. That was all I wanted for you, to get better. I also want you to know I'm not mad anymore. I hated you for so long, but I let it go. Dad, I forgive you."

Raymond Jacobs eyes filled with sadness. His lower eyelids were red with unshed tears. "Thank you," came a quiet whisper.

"I'm glad we got to talk." Emmaline was done. She didn't want to sit and make small talk. She grabbed her purse and started scooting out of the booth.

"Can I see you again?" He looked at her with a glimmer of hope in his eyes.

"We'll see what happens moving forward." With that she turned and left nodding her head at Jim in passing.

Emmaline walked out of the diner lighter in her heart. She headed toward Jay's truck. She watched him get out and walk toward her. "How did it—" She blocked his sentence with a kiss, followed up with a tight hug.

She held him tight, placing her head in her spot on his chest. He held onto her while gently rubbing the hair on her head.

They walked hand in hand to her side of the truck. He helped her up into the seat before walking to his side and climbing. "Do you want to tell me how it went?"

"I will, but not now. I need to sit with it for a bit. I will tell you it went better than I thought, and I didn't yell at him." Emmaline glanced back over at the large windows of the diner to the spot where the table was that she sat at with her father. She could see Jim had taken her spot across from her father. She didn't even care what they were talking about. She was happy she got to say what she needed to say. She wasn't afraid of him anymore. The little girl in her could be free.

Jay cleared his throat drawing her attention back to him. "While you were in the diner, I opened the envelope from Heather. I read the note and know what our homework is. Are you open for a little outing?"

She smiled over at him. "Yes."

Jay drove them through town. He stopped at a grocery store, ran inside, and came out with a bouquet of flowers. "I'm sorry, they aren't for you," he said as he placed the flowers between them, starting the truck back up.

Emmaline watched the world outside go by. She heard Jay turn on his turn signal. She glanced out the window at where they were turning. It was the entrance to Riverside Cemetery in Farmington. "Our homework is to visit a cemetery?"

"You'll see." He parked the truck. "I've actually been here a couple of times, but I couldn't get out of the truck. I think I can with you by my side."

It suddenly occurred to her why they were here. "Is this where..."

"Yes." Jay got out of the truck and walked over to her side. They held hands and walked quietly together past a number of headstones. They walked over to a headstone in a beautiful grassy spot, next to a budding maple tree. Emmaline read the lettering on the granite.

CECELIA DOWNS
JUNE 12, 2007-AUGUST 26, 2024
BELOVED DAUGHTER, SISTER, FRIEND
AN ANGEL ON EARTH
GONE TOO SOON

She watched Jay bend down and place the flowers at the base of the headstone. He placed his hand on her name. "I'm sorry, Cecelia. I'm sorry I lived, and you didn't. I'm sorry you won't get to live the life you were meant to live." He choked up unable to continue. Emmaline moved next to him, crouching down by his side.

"Cecelia, you will be remembered," she said as she kissed her fingertips and placed them on the headstone. Jay was crying next to her.

"I'm sorry, Cecelia. I'm so, so sorry." Emmaline held her husband in her arms as he wept. "It was an accident. It shouldn't have happened. You should be here. We should both be here." His words came out in desperation through sobs. Words he had been needing to say. "I'm sorry I lived, and you didn't."

Emmaline and Jay sat on the ground next to Cecelia's grave crying into each other's arms. All the grief and sadness of the last eight months came pouring out of both of them. The bright rays of the sun appeared from behind the cloudy sky casting its warmth down on their backs.

"Em, can you love me again? This version of me. Can you love *this* Jay?" He nervously looked over at her with hope in his eyes.

She slowly pulled him up to standing. "I already do. I love you, Jay. From this day forward, for better or worse. I give you my heart."

They stood facing each other holding hands. With Cecelia Downs as their witness, they recommitted to each other.

"I love you, Emmaline Ellis. From this day forward, for better or worse, I give you my heart." They sealed their promise with a kiss.

EPILOGUE

Hope is Born

Jay stood outside the door listening to the rustling sounds coming from the other side. His heart was racing with fear and excitement. He felt himself holding his breath and reminded himself to exhale. He closed his eyes, practicing his breathing exercises. He didn't want to get overstimulated and cause himself a migraine. This was way too important of a day to miss out on.

The door to the room gently opened. A nurse in pink scrubs appeared. "Are you ready?"

Jay shook his head slowly, quietly saying, "Yes." He felt like his heart was going to jump out of his body. The nervous anticipation was coursing through him.

The nurse moved out of the way to allow Jay to enter the room. He walked cautiously through the door. The medical team had dimmed the lights, the atmosphere was filled with a quiet stillness. He saw the delivery team around the end of his wife's bed. As he came around the corner, he saw a large sheet draped over the bottom half of her. His eyes found Emmaline's. He walked toward her outstretched hand. She met his eyes with hers, and they both smiled.

"Okay, mama, are you ready to meet your baby," the obstetrician said softly. Jay held Emmaline's hand in his. He placed his other hand gently over the cool cloth on her forehead. Emmaline nodded her head yes at the doctor. Jay took a moment to take it all in. The dim light, the quiet room, the soft words spoken between the medical staff, the beautiful glow on Emmaline's face. All the accommodations were made so he could be here sharing this moment with her. He wished he could pull out his journal and write this moment down in it. He never wanted to forget all of the little details. He looked around in wonder at the miracle happening before him. He turned his gaze down at Emmaline in awe. Her strength over these last weeks of bed rest amazed him. She was already the best mom.

Emmaline squeezed Jay's hand; he could see a glimpse of worry in her eyes. He whispered words of encouragement to her. He glanced over the edge of the curtain as the doctor began to open his wife's belly up. He turned his eyes back to Emmaline. Jay promised her he would not watch as she didn't want him to see her being cut open. Quiet minutes stretched by as the medical staff began the c-section.

"Here she is. You have a baby girl," the doctor said from behind the sheet.

With the umbilical cord still attached the doctor placed their baby in Emmaline's arms. Tears streaked down both of their faces as they stared at their beautiful baby girl. She had Jay's deep brown eyes and a puff of brown hair with the sweetest dimple on her chin.

"Do you have a name picked out?" asked the nurse in the pink scrubs.

"Yes," said Emmaline. "Hope. Hope Cecelia Ellis."

"Hope. What a beautiful name," the nurse replied.

Jay gazed lovingly into Emmaline's eyes. He leaned over, first kissing his daughter and then his wife. He touched his forehead to Emmaline's. "It sure is. Hope is worth fighting for."

ACKNOWLEDGMENTS

Researching and writing this book would not have been possible without the support of some incredibly special people.

Thanks to my writing coach, Jennifer Graybeal, who spent an hour on the phone with me about this story and let me come to my own realization of how it should progress in the last five minutes of our call. I am forever grateful for your guidance.

Amy Briggs, my amazing editor, I can't sing your praises enough. The fact THAT we crossed paths in a Facebook group, THAT led me to reach out to you and THAT you agreed to take me on makes me the luckiest writer. As I keep saying, I am a better writer because of you!

Jennifer Sommerfeld, the incredible narrator for my books, I love sharing this chapter of life with you. Thank you for bringing my stories to listeners with your beautiful voice.

To my cousin, Allison Johnson, thank you for generously sharing your knowledge and gift as a nurse. Your insights allowed me to represent your profession and the work you do with true authenticity.

To my beautiful friend, Monique Hetzler Dallaire, I am beyond grateful for your openness and for sharing your experience as the wife of someone living with a TBI. Your strength and resilience never ceases to amaze me.

Jim Behme at the UConn School of Medicine, your insight into the profound impact of traumatic brain injury on not only the patient but also their caregivers and the medical team has been invaluable. Our conversations have taught me so much, and I cannot imagine Dr. Jim being anything but a reflection of you. Your students are so lucky to have you guiding them into the world of medicine.

Sergeant David Rodriguez of the Canton Police Department. Thank you for sharing your story with me. Your strength, courage and fortitude helped me form Jay into the man I wanted him to be. As I wrote this book, there were countless moments when I felt you were right alongside me helping me guide Jay through his recovery.

To my accountability group who listened week after week as this story took shape and evolved. Corrine Smith, Janet Straightarrow, and Molly Charboneau, I am so blessed that our paths crossed. From bullshit to brilliance, ladies!

To my children, Matthew and Miranda, you are the greatest accomplishments in my life. I am so proud to be your mama.

To Mike, my one and only love, you inspire me every day. I am who I am because I've had you by my side.

QUESTIONS AND TOPICS FOR DISCUSSION

1. The title of the book, *From This Day Forward*, represents a shift in Jay and Emmaline's life. When something unexpected happens in their life they need to learn how they will move forward. Share an experience in your own life where you felt an unexpected shift and how you moved forward from it, either by yourself or with your partner.

2. Who is your favorite character? Who did you most identify with, and why?

3. Mental health serves as a central theme throughout this story, from Emmaline's father's undiagnosed mental illness to Jay's father's addiction stemming from injury to Jay's traumatic brain injury (TBI) and Vivian's dementia. Did you find any part of this relatable? Has mental illness played a role in your life, or the life of someone you love? In Wendy Haller's books she threads the theme of childhood trauma resurfacing in adulthood. Did you relate to that theme in any way, and if so, how?

4. Although family was central to Jay and Emmaline, friendships were also crucial. What do you think friends add to our lives that families don't or can't?

5. Emmaline kept comparing Old Jay to New Jay. Do you think this was fair to Jay or do you think this was her way of processing his TBI and the changes they will need to make for their future together?

6. After finding out her father is still around and lives locally, Emmaline decides she wants to see him. Raymond asks, "Can I see you again?" Emmaline responds, "We'll see what happens moving forward." If you were Emmaline, would you want a relationship with him moving forward and why?

7. Dottie and Andrea are both strong mothers who had to finish raising their children on their own. Reflect on your childhood to a time when you remember one parent having to put aside their own needs and do what is best for their children.

8. Emmaline feels she must do the same when she finds out she's pregnant. If you have children now, can you think of a significant sacrifice you made for one of your children.

ENJOYED *FROM THIS DAY FORWARD*?

Writing this book has been near and dear to me. I loved being a part of Jay and Emmaline's journey as individuals and as a couple. I hope you enjoyed reading it as much as I treasured each moment writing it.

If you enjoyed this story, please consider leaving me a quick review. Please click the stars or post a review on Amazon, Bookbub, and/or Goodreads. Your feedback helps future readers discover my work.

Sign up to receive monthly newsletters with exclusive excerpts, inside scoops, reader polls and fun topics. New subscribers, receive a free copy of my #1 Amazon best seller *Kiss You Love, Goodbye - a poetic journey through life*

Visit me at www.wendyhallerauthor.com.

wendyhaller, author
@wendyhaller_author

Wendy Haller writes across genres. She has published poetry, children's books, and contemporary women's fiction. As a mom and former teacher, Wendy writes her children's books for parents to be used as teachable moments with their kids in a fun and engaging way. Her novels are emotionally driven, coming of age stories with rich dialogue and relatable characters. When not writing she can be found walking in the woods, practicing yoga, or snuggled under a blanket on her couch with a cup of tea and a book. She lives in Connecticut with her husband and two children. Visit her at www.wendyhallerauthor.com.